Lyndsay looked him square in the eye as she said it.

He rubbed one knuckle against the side of his jaw, and let his gaze sweep over her figure in undisguised appreciation. "I'm not denying that. But it might not help me find the treasure."

She poked her finger into his chest. There was no amusement in her face. "Now you see here, Donovan. That's what you get for thinking with your hormones. If you'd spend a few minutes using that part of your brain that's above the waist, it might have occurred to you that I could have a function in life *besides* contributing to your sexual fantasies."

"Sweetheart," he said with a grin, "that may be. But when I'm with you I'm not even sure I have anything above the waist."

ABOUT THE AUTHOR

The versatile Rebecca Flanders is a familiar name to readers of American Romance novels. Since 1983, when she supplied the introductory sampler to the series, she has written over a score of American Romance novels. In addition, she is the author of romantic suspense, mainstream and historical romance novels. Rebecca makes her home in the mountains of Georgia.

Books by Rebecca Flanders

HARLEQUIN AMERICAN ROMANCE
167—AFTER THE STORM
183—PAINTED SUNSETS
257—SEARCH THE HEAVENS
357—THE SENSATION
417—UNDER THE MISTLETOE
454—ONCE UPON A TIME
477—THE LAST REAL MAN

HARLEQUIN INTRIGUE
8—SILVER THREADS
13—EASY ACCESS

HARLEQUIN SUPERROMANCE
180—THE GROWING SEASON

Don't miss any of our special offers. Write to us at the following address for information on our newest releases.

Harlequin Reader Service
P.O. Box 1397, Buffalo, NY 14240
Canadian address: P.O. Box 603,
Fort Erie, Ont. L2A 5X3

Rebecca Flanders

SUNCHASERS

Harlequin Books

TORONTO • NEW YORK • LONDON
AMSTERDAM • PARIS • SYDNEY • HAMBURG
STOCKHOLM • ATHENS • TOKYO • MILAN
MADRID • WARSAW • BUDAPEST • AUCKLAND

Published June 1993

ISBN 0-373-16490-4

SUNCHASERS

Chapter One

She did not know why the appearance of the stranger surprised her. She had felt his approach like a storm on the wind for days now.

Lyndsay Blake would be the last person in the world to believe in precognition, but sometimes she sensed things. A crawling in her skin, a restlessness in the air, a kind of itching at the back of her neck— those were the symptoms that invariably presaged change, the advent of something important. Lyndsay looked up from wiping off the counter after the last of the lunch crowd had departed and she saw him there, silhouetted against the square of light from the open door, and she knew two things: the waiting was over, and this man was trouble.

She thought, *Wow. Somebody should get this on film*. On second thought, she realized somebody already had—several hundred times.

He stood with the light behind him and his shadow stretched across the floor, long and lean in battered boots and Stetson, his features in shadow, looking like he just stepped out of the climactic scene of a Western film. All he needed was a six-gun on his hip and everyone in the place would have been diving for cover.

All he wore on his hips, however, was a pair of very well-fitted jeans which, Lyndsay noticed as he moved into the room and out of the glare of the sun, were no dustier than that of any other patron she had served that day. He swept off his hat to reveal a head of thick brown hair, now compressed from the weight of the hat and damp and curling at the forehead. His jaw was covered with a dark stubble, his eyes were green and as sharp as flint.

"Now there's one cowboy who can put his boots under my bed anytime." Lyndsay had almost forgotten Darlene, the part-time day waitress, until she spoke.

Lyndsay gave her a sharp look and Darlene pushed through the swinging door to the kitchen with a tray of dirty dishes in hand. The rules were clear, and technically Lyndsay had seen him first.

The stranger had seen her, too, and from the way his gaze had lingered on her before moving, somewhat perfunctorily it seemed, to look around the room, Lyndsay could tell he liked what he saw. This was not unusual. Lyndsay was accustomed to the lingering gazes she invariably elicited from men of all descriptions, and she had long since learned to appreciate them for what they were worth. What was somewhat more unusual was that such a gaze, familiar as it was, could make her skin prickle, stirring a kind of excitement within her that was not at all familiar. This man was the most exciting thing she had seen in recent memory.

Of course, she had been stuck out here with nothing but cacti and sagebrush for company for a long time.

Her heart stammered a beat as those eyes completed their brief survey of the interior of the café—which was undistinguished at best—and came to rest on her. He moved toward the counter.

Lyndsay put the sponge on the shelf beneath the counter, instinctively straightening her shoulders and turning on a slow smile. She liked to watch the way his eyes drifted toward the front of her uniform when she did that.

"Howdy, stranger," she said. She brought up a plastic-covered menu and set it on the counter before him. "What can I get for you?"

Jed Donovan moved forward cautiously, reminding himself of the business that had brought him here and trying not to stare too obviously. Sometimes life was good. Sometimes the end of a hot dusty trail held a long cool drink and a tall, statuesque blond waitress with enough sex appeal for ten ordinary women.

Sometimes, of course, it was nothing but a mirage. Jed had run into more than his share of mirages lately, so he was careful about taking this as a sign his luck was changing. But he could hope.

"Ma'am."

His tone was polite, his drawl low and quiet. Lyndsay noted it didn't match his eyes at all.

"I'm looking for a Dr. Blake. Oliver Haywood Blake. They told me at the post office to check over here." He glanced once more at the empty tables behind him. "Maybe you can help me out."

Lyndsay turned with what she hoped was a perfectly casual gesture to fill a glass with water from the serving pitcher at the end of the counter. Her heart was beating hard, even as her mind raced in several dozen directions.

She noticed abruptly that the kitchen, generally a cacophony of boisterous voices, clattering pots and raucous rock and roll, was tomb silent. She was not surprised to glimpse out of the corner of her eye both Duke and Darlene watching with unabashed curiosity through the glass pane in the swinging door. They didn't have too much excitement in their lives, either.

The sight of them restored her composure, but it was with a carefully disguised sense of wariness that Lyndsay turned back to the stranger and set the glass of water before him. "Maybe you'd like to order something."

"I'm not hungry."

She waited.

Finally he said, "Draft beer, frosted glass?"

A flicker of amusement touched the corner of her mouth. "Sorry."

Strike one, Jed thought. "Pie and coffee?"

Lyndsay took the glass dome off a plate of apple pie and cut a slice. Her tone was conversational when she asked, "What do you want with Dr. Blake?"

Jed relaxed, settling his hat on the counter beside him as he slid easily into his spiel. "He's a colleague. Actually we've never met, but we're in the same field. I read a paper of his on the Anasazi and was impressed with some of his theories. My specialty is the American West."

Lyndsay placed the pie before him and poured a cup of coffee. "You're an archaeologist?"

"Jed Donovan," he replied, those ice-sharp eyes never wavering. "I'm a professor at the University of Chicago."

Lyndsay smiled, poured a second cup of coffee, then surprised him by pulling a stool out from her side of the counter and sitting down, cup in hand.

"Well, Mr. Donovan," she said, "you may indeed have attended the University of Chicago—although somehow I doubt even that—but I can promise you have never taught there."

She sipped her coffee. "No self-respecting archaeologist living today would even nod to Oliver Blake on the street, much less look him up for consultation. But you did do your research, I'll grant you that—he did write a rather coherent paper on the

Anasazi, about thirty years ago, while he was still publishable, of course.''

Her voice hardened just a fraction. ''Now who the hell are you, and what do you want?''

Jed Donovan didn't flinch. Lyndsay had to admire a man who could lie to a woman's face, fail miserably, get caught and not even blink.

''Maybe I could ask you the same thing,'' he said.

She took a sip of her coffee, and smiled again. ''I'm Lyndsay Blake. Oliver Blake's daughter.''

Strike two, Jed thought. Several million genuine waitresses in the world, and he had to stumble across the one who could poke holes in his story before the words were even out of his mouth. But Blake's *daughter?* Who the hell would've figured that?

Of course, if even half his brain had been working, he would have known from the minute he walked in the door that she didn't belong in a dive like this, slinging hash. But when a man's eyes were riveted on a figure that should have been in a center-fold and legs that went on twice as long as any woman's legs had a right to and a thick braid of golden blond hair that, even in its disarranged state, made a man picture it spilling through his hands and spread across his pillow.... With all that pulsing through his mind, his thoughts—if he thought at all—tended toward the basic.

He hadn't exactly been tuned in to the subtleties. Eyes that were far too intelligent to belong to that sex-kitten body, movements that, aside from oozing sensuality, were confident and relaxed, a voice that was pleasant and well educated… Nothing about her fit the waitress uniform, and if he had been paying closer attention he would have noticed right away.

Blake's daughter. What the hell was she doing here, in this dust hole of a town in the middle of the Arizona desert, masquerading as a waitress? And more importantly, how much trouble was she going to cause him?

He turned on his most charming smile—the one that had been melting female hearts and loosening female clothing since he was sixteen—and decided the best approach most definitely would *not* be the direct one. With a glance around to indicate their surroundings, he said sympathetically, "Guess the professor's fallen on hard times, huh?" He raised the pie-laden fork to his mouth.

"You could say that." Her expression did not change as she sipped her coffee. "He's dead."

Jed's hand froze in midmotion. The simple pronouncement, uttered so matter-of-factly and without emotion, struck him like a hammer blow in the pit of his stomach. Dead. How could he be *dead?*

It had taken him six months to talk himself into looking up Dr. Blake, a last desperate chance taken by a man who didn't have too many options left. Another three months had been spent tracking him down; he'd worked out his story, driven all the way down here from Oklahoma … and Blake was dead. *Dead.*

Strike three . . . you're out!

What he wanted to do was throw something, kick something, shout at the top of his lungs while invoking every four-letter word he knew. What he said was "When?"

She looked just the smallest bit surprised. "A year ago last January."

Almost eighteen months. Blake had been dead before Jed even began his search.

Wouldn't he ever catch a break? Just one small break?

He looked at the fork in his hand, and at the woman sitting across from him. He let the fork rest on the plate and said, belatedly, "I'm sorry."

Lyndsay shrugged, watching him curiously. "So am I."

He dug into his pocket and tossed two bills on the counter. "Thanks for the coffee." He started to rise.

Lyndsay was not about to let the most interesting thing that had happened to her in over a year just get up and walk out the door. For a moment she couldn't believe he would even try.

"Hey," she called, "what did you want him for anyway?"

Jed might not have stopped to reply, but she chose that moment to bend forward nonchalantly, running her fingertips over one slightly outstretched leg as though checking her stocking for snags. Only she wasn't wearing stockings; Jed could see that immediately. It was, however, a magnificent leg—richly tanned, smooth as silk, completely naked. She arched her foot in the battered white sneaker and Jed could see the curl of her toes. His throat went dry.

He said, "What?"

"My father." She straightened up at leisure, trailing her hand back up the length of her leg and then away. She took another sip of her coffee. "And don't tell me you just wanted to talk shop, because I think we've already established you wouldn't know where to begin. Did he owe you money?"

He reached for his hat, giving a little shake of his head as though to clear the cobwebs. "No."

"You're not a process server, are you?"

"Of course not."

"Then what did you want?"

He gave her a small, patronizing smile. "Well, it really doesn't matter now, does it?"

Lyndsay returned his smile. "No, I suppose not. However..."

Jed stopped.

"I *am* my father's daughter, and we worked very closely together. Maybe I could help you."

There was a note of dry dismissal in his tone as he said, "Being the kind of specialist your father was, I really doubt that, don't you?"

He felt like a fool for coming. He felt like a fool for staying. But he hesitated before putting his hat on his head, and her next words were all the persuasion he needed.

"Finish your pie," Lyndsay suggested, gesturing him to be seated again. "After all, you paid for it."

After only another moment Jed tossed his hat onto the counter and sat down again. "Yeah, I guess you're right."

"Sure I can't get you something else? I'll bet you didn't stop for lunch, and Oklahoma's a long drive."

Jed froze with his fork in midair. "How did you—"

She gestured toward the window. "That's your blue pickup, isn't it? I can see the plates."

He put down the fork, relaxing visibly, and a teasing glint came into her eyes as she surveyed him over the rim of her cup. "Don't tell me you believe in psychics, Mr. Donovan."

He scowled sharply. "Of course not."

"Then why did you come to see my father?"

The scowl deepened, and he muttered, "Hell, I've been asking myself that for the past six months. Not that it matters now."

"Tell me about it," she invited.

Jed hesitated. He was tired. He'd been driving twelve hours straight and the last time he'd eaten had been sometime yesterday. He didn't even know where he was going once he left this café, and he must be crazy to even think of passing up an opportunity to sit and look at scenery like this.

On the other hand, it had been hard enough to think straight when she was walking around pouring his coffee and acting like a waitress. Now that she

Chapter Two

Lyndsay narrowly avoided choking on her coffee. There was a crash in the kitchen that drew Jed's startled glance but she barely noticed it. It was a long time before she could make her voice work.

"That's quite a loss," she managed. She couldn't stop staring at him. And she'd thought he was a bill collector!

Jed was amused as he sipped his coffee. "You could say that."

On the other hand, Lyndsay reminded herself with some effort, he still *could* be a bill collector—or just about anything else. He wouldn't be the first smooth-talking, good-looking con man to cross her path, and if there was one thing life with her father had taught her, it was that the woods were full of them. She deliberately reactivated her skepticism.

She brought the coffee cup to her lips again, watching him over its rim. "How could you have been so careless, I wonder?"

Jed smiled. It was a funny thing—rarely was he tempted to talk about this, certainly never casually and never to a stranger. It didn't matter how sexy the woman was, how inviting her smile or how appealing her other features were—though Jed had to admit he couldn't recall ever having been this close to a woman with features quite as appealing as hers. But with Lyndsay Blake, it was different.

Maybe it was because, by virtue of her relationship to Oliver Blake, she wasn't really a stranger. Maybe he was beginning to doubt whether he really had a secret worth guarding anymore. Maybe it was because, with Blake gone, he was very close to the end of his rope and none of the old rules seemed to apply.

Whatever the reason, he heard himself replying, "First I had a great-grandfather who was foolish enough to get himself killed before he could tell anybody where he hid it."

Lyndsay lifted an eyebrow. "That *was* inconsiderate of him."

Jed gave a snort of laughter. "Tell me about it."

Lyndsay eyed him thoughtfully, and decided that a woman would be a fool to believe a word he said. That square, dark-stubbled jaw, those full lips, that rumpled, tumbled-down hair... The only thing missing was a dimple in his chin, and Lyndsay found herself taking some small reassurance in that. She never had trusted perfection and Jed Donovan was perilously close to that. Fortunately, Lyndsay had always found his particular brand of low-and-lazy, rough-and-tumble sex appeal easy to resist.

For the most part.

Usually.

Well . . . sometimes.

She got up to replenish his coffee, and her own. "Who was this absentminded ancestor of yours, anyway?"

"His name was Joshua Running Horse. He was a Creek chief."

"He made his money in commodities, no doubt."

"Real estate."

He lifted the refilled cup in one brown, work-roughened hand and gazed at her over the steam. There was an appreciative spark of amusement in his eye that Lyndsay found hard to resist.

"As a matter of fact," he went on easily, "he might well have been one of the first—and most successful—brokers the Creeks ever produced."

He took a sip of the coffee, and again Lyndsay was gratified by the way his eyes followed her movements as she resumed her seat on the stool, crossing her legs, straightening the hem of her skirt.

"He sounds like an interesting fellow," she said. "But I don't understand what he has to do with my father."

Jed found his thoughts wandering to legends he had heard of man-eating jungle plants. Lush, succulent, deadly in their allure, lying in wait for the careless and unaware. He shook his head and focused his attention on the subject at hand.

"Joshua negotiated with the U.S. government to reimburse the tribe for lands it had confiscated," he explained, "and he actually won. It wasn't the only time the government paid the Indians for what they'd stolen, but it was one of the few times they paid a fair price."

His voice softened just a fraction and far back in his eyes was a dreamy, hungry look that Lyndsay had no difficulty at all recognizing as he added, "All in gold, U.S. government mint. Nothing to sneeze at even back then, but by today's standards worth two and a half million. At least."

Lyndsay tried to conceal her disappointment. A treasure hunter. Just a plain, ordinary, run-of-the-mill treasure hunter. And he had seemed so much smarter than that.

No, she corrected herself mentally. He had seemed so much more *interesting* than that.

And she still wasn't quite ready to let him go.

"You don't look Creek," she said.

It took him half a beat to drag his attention away from the past and back to her again; Lyndsay saw it in his eyes and was intrigued. It wasn't often she was on the losing end of any kind of competition for a man's attention, and if this fantasy treasure of his was that important to him, it might not hurt to hear more about it.

He shrugged. "I guess by now I'm not. Old Joshua's daughter married a white man, and so on and so on down the line, until here I am—" he grinned suddenly, devastatingly "—full of Irish charm and handsome as sin."

Lyndsay couldn't help smiling back. Had she only a moment ago classified him as *ordinary?* No one with a grin like that could be called ordinary.

"And full of blarney, too, no doubt."

The small laugh lines around his eyes deepened as he answered in a thick brogue, "Well now, me darlin', I'll not be arguin' that with a lady as pleasin' to the eye as yourself, now will I?"

Lyndsay laughed. "I like a man who goes with his best pitch."

The spark in his eyes held more than a hint of promise as he replied softly, "Honey, you haven't even *seen* my best pitch yet."

Lyndsay found herself unable—or perhaps unwilling—to draw her gaze away from his. A tingle of excitement coursed down her spine and she was gripped by a sudden, urgent curiosity to know what his best pitch was.

It was with an effort that she kept her tone casual. "So how did he lose the money? In a card game?"

This time his grin was wonderfully crooked, and the slight shake of his head conceded a small victory to her in the everlasting battle of the sexes.

"Bandits," he replied. "There was lots of speculation about whether it was all a setup from the beginning, but he was ambushed on the way back with the gold. He was killed in the attack, but not before taking two of the three men out with him. When the last one went in for the loot, it was gone. Joshua must've known what the odds were of his getting out alive, and he hid the cask of gold."

"Or the robber was lying," Lyndsay pointed out. She knew it was none of her business and she wasn't even interested but she couldn't stop her mind from working. The inability to resist exposing stupidity wherever she found it was, she liked to think, one of her few vices.

"Who takes the word of a bandit, anyway?" she asked. "Or maybe Joshua never had any gold at all. Maybe he sent it by a different route, which would've been the smart thing to do. Maybe he made the whole thing up to look like a big shot before the tribe. I don't mean to criticize, Donovan, but most treasure hunts start with a much stronger theory than this."

He smiled faintly. "Which is probably why this particular treasure has stayed hidden for almost a hundred and fifty years."

Generally, that was where he would have stopped—if he had even got that far. He should leave it at that. He hadn't felt the need to impress a woman since high school, and it wasn't that adolescent urge that motivated him now. But he had come here to tell a story. What difference did it make whether he told it to the father or the daughter? Neither one of them could help him now.

And it wasn't as though he had any intention of telling the *whole* truth. Not even for a figure like hers.

"Matter of fact," he said, "that's what most people thought at the time, too. But that bandit was caught during a bank robbery a few months later and went to prison. He talked about going back to look for that man's gold until the day he died—in prison, ten years later. I don't think he would've been robbing a bank if he *had* had the money, and he sure wouldn't have been talking about it in prison."

Jed paused for effect, sipping his coffee. "Then, fifty years later, a witness came forward. He saw Joshua hide the money before the ambush."

"The plot thickens," murmured Lyndsay sarcastically. Truth was, she was no more immune to the allure of a good mystery than anyone else, and it was beginning to sound as though this man might actually have something.

His eyes twinkled. "So it does. Anyway, to make a long story short, based on that eyewitness account I was able to construct a map. The trouble is, of course, after a hundred and fifty years the landmarks have changed or disappeared, so all I've got is a general area—pretty broad as a matter of fact."

Lyndsay nodded somewhat absently. Her ears had pricked up at the word *map* and her mind was working quickly. "And you thought my father could narrow it down for you."

He lifted one shoulder in a gesture of light dismissal. "It was worth a shot."

But the look in his eyes belied his casual tone, and there was no disguising it: pure, unadulterated greed, seasoned with just a dash of desperation. Lyndsay had seen that look too many times in the mirror to mistake it on anyone else.

"It must be pretty important to you," she said.

"Just a hobby, really. Since it's kind of a family matter, I enjoy trying to piece it together in my spare time. As for your father... well, I'd never met a psychic archaeologist before, and I thought it'd be kind of wild. Add spice to the stories I tell when I'm old and gray, you know."

Lyndsay returned the smile that had no doubt slayed a thousand females before her and she thought, *Liar.*

He might or might not be a hobbyist; the truth was he didn't look as though he could afford to devote full-time to treasure hunting. But this was more to him than just a chance to get outdoors on weekends with a metal detector, more than just something to do with his "spare time." If Lyndsay had thought that to be the case, she would have dismissed his story without another thought. If it hadn't been for that look in his eyes, she would have shrugged him off as just another dream chaser.

But he might really have a map. And if he did . . .

Her tone revealed only the mildest curiosity as she inquired, "Where did you hear about my father?"

"Here and there," he said. "There was that article about his part in uncovering that Ute village, and one of the archaeology magazines mentioned him being on the scene of one of the dinosaur digs in Colorado."

Lyndsay wondered if it were tact or technique on his part that led him to mention two of Oliver Blake's earliest associations which, even though still hotly debated in the academic community, were the only two examples of his work that could be even remotely construed as respectable.

No mere hobbyist, of course, would have taken the trouble to research obscure archaeology magazines from over twenty years ago. Lyndsay's curiosity increased another degree.

She gave him a faintly condescending smile. "Of course," she acknowledged, "most of what has been written about my father is far less flattering. I'm surprised it wasn't one of the tabloids you picked up on."

Donovan looked at her for a moment, then reached into his shirt pocket. "As a matter of fact, it was."

He brought out a folded square of newsprint and handed it to her. It was slightly damp from his body heat and worn along the creases from much handling; Lyndsay unfolded it carefully and winced at what she saw.

It was an inside page from one of those supermarket rags; one that Lyndsay, thankfully, had never

seen. Sandwiched between the headlines, Woman
Gives Birth To Alien Twins and Farmer Raises 32-
Pound Tomato was a grainy picture of her father,
standing with his hands outstretched over a piece of
undistinguished-looking ground, looking stupefied
or drugged the way people usually did in those pho-
tographs. The caption read Psychic Archaeologist
Declares, There's Untold Wealth Beneath This
Ground!

Lyndsay could tell at a glance that the dowsing rod
his hands had been holding had been scrubbed from
the picture. She doubted whether, in fact, he had ever
even been to the area of the country depicted by the
photograph, although in his later years he had traveled quite a bit in connection with his "water-
dowsing" business. Some people would pay for
anything.

She was quite certain her father had never said
anything remotely resembling the tabloid quote.

She scanned the one paragraph article briefly.
"Noted psychic archaeologist Oliver Haywood Blake
is on the trail of yet another fantastic treasure, re-
porters learned Friday...." It was the usual non-
sense, half exaggeration, half total fiction. Reading
it embarrassed Lyndsay, infuriated her, brought forth
her sharpest defensive instincts ... and all for a man
who no longer needed her to protect him.

It was several moments before she trusted herself
to refold the paper and return it to Jed without being tempted to shred it first. Still, it was an effort to

keep her voice mild as she inquired, "Do you believe everything you read, Mr. Donovan?"

"No," he answered, and tucked the paper back into his pocket. "But did you happen to notice that little rise across the highway, over his left shoulder in the picture? That was one of the boundaries on my map. Just seemed like too much of a coincidence to ignore, that's all."

For the first time since he had begun his story, Lyndsay was speechless. More than that, she was genuinely impressed. So much so that for a moment she couldn't even think of a reason not to believe him.

He glanced at his watch. "Well. It's getting late." He reached for his hat. "Pleasure meeting you. Thanks again for the coffee."

He got to his feet. Lyndsay practically jumped to hers, setting the coffee cup on the counter with a clatter. Her mind was racing.

"Wait," she said quickly, then could have bitten her tongue out for sounding so eager. But there were too many possibilities here—not the least of which was Jed Donovan himself—for her to let him just slip through her fingers.

He looked a little surprised at the urgency in her tone, and she swiftly readjusted her approach. Her expression softened, her voice dropped a notch in timbre, and she tilted her head just so, adopting a sultry air.

"I mean," she said, "you're not really starting back now, are you? In the heat of the day, after such a long drive?" She moved slowly around the counter toward him, smiling. "Why don't you stay over and get a fresh start in the morning?"

A slow smile curved his lips as he met her eyes. "Well, now, little darlin', that's not to say I wouldn't enjoy sitting here watching you, but something tells me I'd just be wasting my time. Wouldn't I?"

Lyndsay moved a little closer, holding his gaze. Something about the way he said that caused her pulse to catch for half a beat. "That depends on what you want for your time."

He looked her over once more, toe to eyelashes, slowly and completely, and with a kind of speculative interest that made Lyndsay's heart beat a little faster. "I reckon I ought to think about that one for a while," he said.

"I reckon you should. And while you're thinking, there's a motel right down the street there, due west. It's not much but the sheets are clean and the roaches aren't too big."

"Maybe I should ask what you're offering."

Everything about Jed Donovan was thrilling, Lyndsay thought. Intriguing, bold, exciting, even a little dangerous. How long had it been that just standing near a man like this could make her blood race?

She moved a little closer. "What I'm offering, Mr. Donovan, is—among other things—my help with your project."

His eyes rested on her mouth just long enough to make the nerve endings there actually tingle in anticipation, then drifted lower. "I think I'm more interested in the other things." He raised his eyes to hers again. "But I'll take whatever help I can get. What did you have in mind?"

"I can't promise you anything, but my father kept an extensive diary—impressions that came to him, clues he never had a chance to follow up. When you were telling your story, it sounded familiar to me, which might mean my father had mentioned parts of it to me before. And if he really was where that photograph seems to place him...well, maybe he did get something, and maybe he wrote it down. I could check for you."

Lyndsay's father had not kept a diary. He had not, in fact, even been organized enough to keep a calendar.

Fortunately, Lyndsay was adept at improvisation—a skill she had acquired fending off her father's bill collectors—and Jed Donovan obviously needed a little extra persuasion to stay.

The spark of interest in his eyes kindled with a swiftness that Lyndsay found vaguely disappointing. She would have much preferred, as would any woman, if that light were reserved solely for her charms.

"Is that a fact?" he said.

She gave a modest shrug. "Like I said, I can't promise anything but..." And she turned on her most devastating smile. "It might be worth buying a lady dinner for."

She was gratified then to see that spark glow into embered coals, and this time it was reserved entirely for her. He admitted, "It just might at that."

"Good. There's a little Tex-Mex place in front of the motel. I'll meet you there. Is six too early?"

"Sounds fine."

He didn't move. Neither did she.

She dragged her eyes from his, down his chest to the strongest pair of thighs she had ever seen. A day that had started out as dull as dust was beginning to hold more promise all the time, she thought.

When Lyndsay looked back at his face, she was not surprised to find his eyes had been roaming, too. She repressed a smile. "Until six then."

One corner of his lips lifted ruefully as he put his hat on. "Right."

He turned to go.

"By the way..." Lyndsay called after him.

He looked back.

"They're real."

His eyes returned to her chest, and then met hers with a wink. "So are mine," he said.

Lyndsay grinned as she watched him walk out the door. Whether anything came of his treasure story or not, she had a feeling Jed Donovan would definitely bear further investigation.

Chapter Three

Lyndsay was still gazing in pleasured speculation at the empty doorway when a male voice, soft with admiration, spoke beside her. "Way to go, Lyns."

"You have all the luck," Darlene added, not quite as generously.

"To each his own, Darlene." Duke reprimanded the younger woman. "You, for example, would have been content to get a free dinner out of the poor sap. But our noble leader has something much more ambitious in mind. Don't you, oh, Wise One?"

"Yeah," Darlene muttered. "Dinner *and* a tumble in the sack."

"I resent that," Lyndsay replied mildly. But she had never taken Darlene seriously enough to get upset with her, and she certainly wasn't about to begin now. She had far too much to think about to spare energy on the inconsequential.

"What was all that garbage about buried treasure?" Duke asked. "You don't really think...?"

"I don't know. But since my dance card seems to be empty for the next couple of hours I thought it wouldn't hurt to spend a little time finding out. That is, of course—" meaningfully she arched an eyebrow at him "—if you think you can spare me here."

Duke pulled a long-suffering look. "Well, it'll mean canceling the catered dinner for the Honduran ambassador, but go ahead."

Lyndsay was already heading for the door, but she grinned and stroked Duke's bearded cheek affectionately as she passed. "You're a sweetheart."

On her way out she heard Darlene protesting, "What ambassador? Are we opening for dinner?"

And Duke's soothing reply, "Never mind, Cinderella, back to the pots and pans."

Lyndsay had known Duke and Darlene for two years, ever since her father's last wild scheme had stranded her here. Duke, a former minor-league baseball star, was now owner, manager and chief chef of the Trail's End Café. Darlene was one of his strays, just as, Lyndsay supposed, she herself was. It was odd to think that these two people, with whom she had nothing at all in common, were now her closest friends in the world. Odder still to realize that she had been in this truck stop on the edge of nowhere for two years now.

Lyndsay didn't have far to go. She exited the front door, took a right and climbed a set of stairs that led to the flat rooftop of the Trail's End. The gravelly rooftop was a natural mirror for the sun's rays, and it was bright enough to blind. She could feel the heat through the soles of her sneakers, but had learned to walk quickly so her shoes wouldn't melt.

The fifteen-by-fifteen rooftop apartment was part of her deal with Duke—that and thirty percent of the gross bought her services as waitress, bookkeeper and day manager for the Trail's End. It had seemed like a good deal when Lyndsay had taken it, claiming, "Just until I got back on my feet"—a couple of months at best. But two years... It struck her again as she pushed open the door of the little building. How could she have been here two years?

The temperature inside the apartment was only a few degrees cooler than the desert air outside, despite the air conditioner that bravely chugged away in the window over the bed. A former tenant— Lyndsay suspected it might have been Duke himself, during what he called his "earth child" period—had painted the walls mud red and covered the windows and bed with a now-faded batik print, and Lyndsay had not bothered to change the decor. She simply hadn't expected to be here long enough to bother, and besides, she had never cared much about the appearance of her surroundings. In fact, she couldn't really say she'd ever even noticed... until now.

She kicked off her shoes the minute she crossed the threshold, and was unbuttoning her uniform as she crossed to the bar-size refrigerator for a soda. She kept the room dark to ward off the heat, but she had never noticed before how depressing that was. A twin bed, a chest of drawers, a thirteen-inch black-and-white television with a tin-foil antenna, a bathroom that was barely big enough to turn around in . . . Her entire wardrobe, such as it was, was piled on a ladder-back chair or hung from a hook on the back of the door. Hadn't she expected to be in Cairo by now?

Hadn't she expected to be *somewhere* by now?

She pulled the tab on her soda and sat down cross-legged on the bed, fanning the open collar of her uniform in hopes of catching a breath of tepid air from the air conditioner. For a moment she hesitated. Of all the crazy strangers with all their wild tales that had crossed her path in the past ten years, why should she choose to believe this one?

But *two years*. Where had the time gone? Where was her *life* going? This particular stranger might be her last chance for a ticket out of here. It was certainly worth a phone call to find out.

She reached for her address book and thumbed through it purposefully until she found the number she wanted. Less than a minute later the dry tones of Dr. Jeffrey Gray greeted her.

"Well, if it isn't the estimable Ms. Blake, foremost authority on the prehistoric Southwest. I assume you're calling to invite me to the Nobel Prize ceremonies."

"Good to hear your voice, too, Jeffrey."

Jeffrey was an ex-professor and an ex-boyfriend from her UCLA days; they kept in touch sporadically because the world of archaeology was small and one never knew who was going to come in handy, but also because, despite herself, Lyndsay liked him. He was a man who, like her father, had all the potential for greatness and one fatal flaw. Her father's flaw had been dream chasing, Jeffrey's was alcohol. No matter how she tried, Lyndsay couldn't seem to shake the knack she had for surrounding herself with losers.

"Damn it, Lyndsay, you're not still sitting out there in the desert pouring coffee for truck drivers and bean farmers, are you?"

Lyndsay rubbed the cold can across her forehead, sipped from it, then pressed it against her neck. "Yep."

"What is it with you Blakes? A recessive gene that compels you to waste your lives?"

For some reason, that made Lyndsay bristle. "This from a guy who's one step away from giving guided tours of the Grand Canyon for tips! Shall we talk about wasted lives, Jeffrey?"

A pause, and Lyndsay wondered with a stab of guilt if she had gone too far. Then she heard his low chuckle. "It's good to hear your voice, Lyns. Now what do you want?"

Lyndsay wasted no further time. "What do you know about a Joshua Running Horse and a lost strongbox full of gold?"

She could practically see his eyes light up. "U.S. mint?"

"You bet."

"Tell me more."

Lyndsay did.

"NOTED PSYCHIC archaeologist Oliver Haywood Blake is on the trail of yet another fantastic treasure..."

Jed studied the clipping for another moment, as he had done so many times before over the past few years, then refolded the paper and tossed it onto the scarred motel room dresser to rest beside his wallet and car keys. Psychic archaeologist. Who was he kidding?

"Man, if you're not careful, you're going to get as crazy as everyone thinks you are," he muttered with a disgusted shake of his head.

Already he was talking to himself. That was not a good sign.

Jed Donovan was not a man who believed in miracles, lucky breaks or even the easy way out. He had worked too hard all his life and had gotten too little to start counting on help from supernatural quarters at this late date. And it wasn't as though he'd been counting on anything, exactly. It was just that when he'd seen that picture...

The article had come to his attention through a co-worker who knew of his "treasure-hunting" hobby. One didn't spend as much money as he did on high-tech electronic devices without the word getting out, but no one knew that he sought a specific treasure, or that he was anyplace close to finding it. The co-worker had tossed him that tabloid with a comment like, "Now there's a guy who can save you a lot of trouble!" And the coincidence was too much to ignore.

Why had a self-proclaimed psychic archaeologist picked Jed's parcel of earth to stand on when he declared "There's untold wealth beneath this ground!"?

Jed didn't have the entire answer, but the basis of it was fairly clear. Psychic? Hardly. But Blake had headed several respectable digs in the American West. It was possible he had stumbled upon the story of Joshua Running Horse. It was possible he had stumbled upon more than that.

It was possible the whole thing was some kind of scam. But Jed had to find out.

And there was only one way to do that—seek out Dr. Oliver Haywood Blake himself.

But even then, Jed's skepticism had held strong. He had read what he could find about the so-called science of psychic archaeology and had remained unimpressed. But the curiosity wouldn't let him go. Why had Blake chosen that particular piece of ground upon which to make his dramatic pronouncement?

Even when his letters to Blake went unanswered, his curiosity had grown—just as his alternatives, and his bank account, diminished.

So here he was with an incomplete treasure map, a dead psychic archaeologist and a woman who could have given Mata Hari lessons in seduction. And once again it was his curiosity that kept him here. If Blake were on the level—at least as far as the archaeologist in him was concerned—the diary might prove to be valuable. If the whole thing was a scam, his daughter was in it as deep as he had ever been, and that was something Jed definitely intended to find out.

But he had little faith in the diary angle; that wasn't why he stayed. Lyndsay Blake, with her centerfold body and her steamy sex appeal and a mind like a steel trap... now *she* was worth staying for. It was certainly worth giving away a harmless secret or two, just to find out what she was up to. Already he suspected she was as big a scam artist as her father probably was. But if not...

His lips curved into a satisfied smile as he sat down on the bed to tug off his boots. If not, he might well have stumbled onto the proverbial gold mine. And that was *definitely* worth hanging around to find out.

Either way, he had nothing to lose but time. And time, unfortunately, was the one thing he seemed to have more than enough of these days.

IT WAS A QUARTER till six when Jeffrey called her back. Lyndsay snatched up the phone without a greeting.

"It's about time!"

"Hey, do you think they keep these things on a central computer? I had to make a few calls." Then, "How did you know it was me?"

Lyndsay replied impatiently, "Come on, what did you find out?" She balanced on one foot to pull on her sandal. "I'm on my way out the door."

"Forgive me. I forgot it's the height of the opera season."

But Jeffrey knew when to stop pushing his luck. "There is a map," he said. "Or there used to be. According to my most excellent sources, it's been underground for almost a hundred years."

Lyndsay paused in the act of fastening a turquoise dangle earring. "Son of a bitch," she exclaimed softly. "He told me *he* drew the map."

"Maybe he did," volunteered Jeffrey. "If so—*de nada*. But if it's the real thing...well, let's just say I was just offered twenty grand for it, sight unseen."

Lyndsay sat down hard on the bed. For a moment her head spun. Twenty thousand dollars. That was Cairo. That was champagne at the top of the pyramid at Giza. That was...

Barely one percent of the value of the treasure.

She swallowed hard and made herself focus. The air conditioner hummed loudly in her ear, but didn't begin to cool the perspiration that suddenly sheened her body. "Then there *is* a treasure."

"Oh, there's a treasure all right. The only question that remains—aside from where, of course—is how much."

"What do you mean? If you were offered twenty thousand..."

"I mean that two and a half million is starting to look like a conservative estimate."

For the second time that day, Lyndsay was speechless.

Jeffrey went on. "You know how it is with these treasure hunters.... It's easier to remove a kidney than drag any information from them. But there's something really interesting going on here, Lyns, and if I were you, the first thing I'd ask myself is just how much of the truth this cowboy of yours told you—which, if he's a typical treasure hunter, wasn't much at all. The second thing I'd ask is, if old Joshua was on his way back to Oklahoma from negotiating with the U.S. government which, last I heard was in Washington, D.C., what was he doing in Colorado?"

Lyndsay's scowl sharpened. "Colorado? Who said anything about Colorado?"

"*My* source," replied Jeffrey a trifle smugly.

Lyndsay hesitated, rubbing the back of her neck tensely. A thousand possibilities cartwheeled through her mind, hundreds of dancing rainbows and each one filled with so much promise, she was dazzled by the light. But Lyndsay knew from experience that to grab at rainbows was to come up with a handful of air and determinedly she focused on the proverbial bird-in-hand.

"But the map," she said. "You're sure there's a market for it?"

Jeffrey's disappointment was eloquently expressed in the brief silence that followed. "That," he replied, "is the tragic result of two years of living among truck drivers and bean farmers. They've stolen your ambition—not to mention your imagination."

Lyndsay glanced impatiently at the bedside alarm clock. "Jeffrey..."

"Twenty thousand is just the broker's fee," he replied. "The finder's fee is usually ten percent of whatever's uncovered—if the map is authentic, of course."

"How do I authenticate it?"

They both knew there were ways to age paper, or even leather or rawhide, that were undetectable to the naked eye, so Jeffrey did not waste time with the obvious. "The original map is called the Widowmaker because one of the triangulation points was a dead tree—the kind that travelers used to give a wide berth because if one of the high branches fell it could impale a man. Another one was, apparently, a forked stream. It's conceivable a forgery might contain one, but not both. And since neither one of those landmarks exists today, if the guy drew the map himself it won't have either one of them."

Lyndsay's heart beat just a fraction faster. Jed had said something about the landmarks on his map no longer being in existence.

But her suspicious nature stirred itself one last time. "For a treasure that's supposed to be so secret, it seems to me an awful lot is known about that map."

Jeffrey chuckled. "Except for a couple of fairly important details. Like *where* in the great state of Colorado this particular dead tree and forked stream were a hundred years ago... and what the third triangulation point was."

"That's why they're putting up the big bucks."

"Right."

"Thanks, Jeff." She started to hang up.

"Lyns?"

She paused.

"Keep in touch, will you? I've got to admit you've got my curiosity up and I'm going to look into this some more. I might have something for you in a few days."

Lyndsay smiled, knowing the possibility of that was extremely remote. One of Jeffrey's problems was his inability to maintain an interest in any project for more than a few hours. He got bored, he started to drink—and everybody lost.

But Lyndsay said gently, "You bet. Take care of yourself, huh?"

"Don't I always?"

Lyndsay didn't really have time to waste before the mirror, and she had a dozen—a hundred—more important things to worry about than her appearance, but she had learned whenever men were involved it was important to keep her priorities straight. It didn't matter whether one was negotiating a trade agreement with a head of state or the freshest fish with a waiter, the advantage invariably belonged to the one with the cleavage. Tonight Lyndsay had a feeling she was going to need every advantage she could get.

Lyndsay had not been born beautiful. She had been born gangly and awkward and too smart for her own good. But by the time she turned sixteen she realized this could be a good thing.

She still wasn't beautiful and she knew it. Her features were strong and Nordic—a handsome face. Though her natural hair color was mouse brown, she wore it blond and it was her one and only vanity.

When men looked at Lyndsay they saw a size thirty-eight bust and full lush hips and legs that wouldn't quit—the stuff of which male fantasies were made. And there were certain rewards to be had from playing into the male fantasy...particularly when the male involved was as interesting as Jed Donovan.

Tonight, with any luck at all, the rewards might go beyond the obvious.

Chapter Four

In an off-the-shoulder peasant blouse and an eyelet Western skirt, a squash-blossom turquoise necklace, bracelet and dangle earrings, Lyndsay was overdressed for the El Rio. But she was only human, after all, and she had more than one reason for wanting to look stunning to Jed Donovan.

The little town of Hapsburg, Arizona, population 890, was anchored on the east by the Trail's End—"Serving Breakfast and Lunch"—and on the west by the Blue Moon Motel/El Rio Mexican Restaurant—"Fine Dining and Cocktails 5:00 p.m. to 10:30 p.m." The drive took four and a half minutes; Lyndsay was five minutes late and she had the most awful feeling that, in those five minutes, Jed Donovan might have gotten away.

He had not. There was nothing subdued about the atmosphere of the El Rio—brightly lit, uncluttered, with a pool table in the back room and a television set over the bar—and he was easy to spot, sitting at a window table and drinking a beer, gazing out at the desert.

When she started toward him, Lyndsay could feel the eyes of every man in the room on her. In only a moment so were Jed's, and she liked the appreciative light she saw there. She smiled as he got to his feet.

"Manners," she said. "I like that in a man."

"Peasant blouse," he returned. "I like that on a woman."

Lyndsay laughed as she sat down. It was the first time she had enjoyed a genuine laugh with a man in...she couldn't remember how long. "Who would've thought a man like you would know what a peasant blouse was?"

"Just goes to show you appearances can be deceiving." And he smiled. "Can't they?"

There was something about his smile that was a little unsettling, and Lyndsay thought perhaps the best response to that would be no response at all.

He had shaved and changed his shirt, but his was the kind of face that would perpetually sport a dark beard shadow—an effect that was only accented by the white, open-necked shirt he wore, and which Lyndsay found as sexy as hell. She wasn't really close enough to smell the soap on his skin—particularly not over the sharp odors of onions and cumin and mesquite smoke coming from the kitchen—but she liked to imagine she could. She liked to imagine the taste of it on his skin, damp and steamy from the shower, and it was enough to make a girl lose her appetite for anything else, and forget business altogether.

She settled back in her chair, trying to appear casual as she crossed her legs under the table. "I guess you're curious."

"You better believe it."

He was still smiling, bottle-green eyes lazy and relaxed as they gazed into her, filled with a dozen things that had nothing whatsoever to do with maps or treasures or psychic archaeologists. Seeing that look in his eyes gave her a little jolt, a thrill of anticipation that was almost electrical in nature. It had been a long time since she had flirted with someone who knew how to do it well.

The waiter paused to set two menus before them, and without looking at him, Lyndsay said, "Draft."

Jed said, "Funny. I would've taken you for the margarita type."

"Wrong. I'm the champagne type."

"That would have been my second guess."

"Do you want to know what I found out?"

Jed wanted to know, badly. For the past four hours he had thought about little else. But he wouldn't let her know just how interested he was.

Oddly, now that she was sitting across from him with that gold-blond hair tumbled across her bare shoulders, smoky gray eyes hiding a multitude of sinful thoughts—at least some of which, he hoped, were about him—Jed found the entire subject of treasure maps and hidden clues somewhat less urgent than it once had been.

He said, "Actually, no. Let's save it for dessert."

She looked surprised, but hid it quickly. Jed felt a twinge of satisfaction.

"So you're into delayed gratification. That I wouldn't have guessed."

"Oh, yes," he admitted, still holding her eyes. "I like to delay it as long as I possibly can. You?"

He saw the long muscles of her throat constrict as she swallowed, and he felt a responsive tightening low in his own belly. The air seemed to thicken between them, becoming charged with pinpoints of awareness.

"That depends," she said.

Her eyes were smoky, the pupils dark. There was a magnetic line between them, holding them on a slow, straight, unwavering collision course toward each other. Neither of them made any effort to veer away.

"On what?"

Her voice sounded husky. "On whether I think it's worth waiting for."

"Oh, it is," he assured her. "I promise you that."

It had become almost a contest of wills, this thing with the eyes, a symbol of sexual potency, a demonstration of seductive power. She had started it, but Jed was confident he would be the one to finish it. And he was right.

A thin veil of color suffused her cheeks, making her eyes as bright as diamonds. She shifted her gaze away. "I wonder if we're talking about the same thing," she murmured.

Jed smiled. "I think so. In fact..." He raised his mug to her in a small salute. "I'm almost sure of it."

The waiter brought her beer, and Lyndsay tried not to reach for it too desperately. Had a man ever been able to raise her temperature by simply talking to her? And she had thought the man had mere possibilities. A masterful understatement.

Jed said, "What's good?"

It took her a moment to understand what he was referring to. Then she noticed the waiter poised purposefully beside their table and she said, distractedly, "Umm—the Juárez Platter."

"Two," Jed said, and the waiter left with a nod.

Lyndsay took a long drink of her beer.

"Interesting necklace," Jed said in a moment.

Lyndsay leaned back in her chair, relaxing a fraction as she fingered the necklace. "It's a copy of an Aztec priest's ceremonial garb. The original was discovered in a tomb in Mexico in 1952. My father gave it to me."

One eyebrow arched slightly. "Only a copy?"

Lyndsay met his gaze with a deliberate smile. "It's against the law to remove artifacts from a country without the permission of the government and appropriate them for personal use. You surely aren't accusing me of doing anything illegal?"

His mild tone left her completely unenlightened about what he thought, and she found that vaguely irritating. "Of course not."

She shrugged. "Anyway, if I had the original, I certainly wouldn't be hanging around this dust heap."

"Which brings me to the first thing I'm curious about." He took a drink from the mug. "What the hell *are* you doing here?"

"Ah, long story time."

"I don't have any pressing appointments, do you?"

Lyndsay smiled. Nothing about this conversation was going the way she had expected, but she had to admit she didn't mind. Jed Donovan, the man who was into delayed gratification, was growing more interesting by the minute.

She saw no reason not to tell him the truth—in this matter, anyway.

"As you may have gathered, my father was particularly interested in the Anasazi—or at least some version of an ancient American superrace, which the Anasazi may or may not have represented, according to my dad." She paused to drink from her mug. "He was convinced that the evidence of the existence of this superrace—maybe even their origins—lay here, in the Four Corners region, and he set up camp about twenty miles outside town to do his research."

"Psychic or archaeological research?"

The question made her instinctively uncomfortable. Then she realized this man was hardly likely to mock what he'd driven across a state to seek out. "A little of both, actually. You know, there actually have been some interesting digs not too far from here that do suggest the existence of an Indian tribe, previous to anything we knew about before."

Jed was not so easily sidetracked. "That explains what your father was doing here. What about you?"

She glanced out the window, where a strip of blacktop bisected the barren desert, flat and featureless, a road leading nowhere. She took another sip of beer, and tried to make her voice as flat as the road.

"His health wasn't particularly good, hadn't been for years. He had no business camping out in the desert in his shape. Besides..." And it was no use, the bitterness crept into her voice as hard as she tried to prevent it. "It might not surprise you to know my father wasn't much of a businessman and someone had to support us while he was out chasing dreams."

Already she was beginning to suspect she had said too much, and a glance at his face confirmed it. Those quick sharp eyes saw entirely too much. She wrapped it up quickly, and in a tone that sounded far too callous, even to her ears.

"Anyway, he had the expected heart attack, left behind a mountain of debts and no insurance, so here I am, waiting tables in this pit stop in hell with not a whole lot better to do."

She lifted her mug again with a false bright salute. "But enough about me. What about you?"

His expression remained pleasant, his eyes steady and much too perceptive. "A woman who doesn't like to talk about herself. Now that's a nice change."

"I like the air of mystery it gives me. Are you a professional treasure hunter?"

His startled laugh seemed genuine, but she almost didn't notice, so entranced was she by the way the light sparked in his eyes.

"What would make you think a thing like that?"

She shrugged, studying him. "Just asking. There are people who make their living that way, you know."

"Can't be much of a living."

She thought he was serious, but the food arrived just then and she didn't have a chance to pursue the subject. Not that it mattered whether he was a professional . . . except if he was really only a hobbyist, she would definitely have the advantage.

Jed ordered another round of beer and eyed the platter before him. "Looks good."

"It's hot." She picked up her fork. "So what are you if you're not a professional treasure hunter?"

"I'm a part-time mechanic, full-time twin-engine pilot—without, unfortunately, a plane."

Lyndsay's brow knit with confusion. "You're a pilot *and* a mechanic? How did that happen?"

"I learned to fly in the army. But when I got out there were more jobs for mechanics than pilots. Particularly," he added with a grin so boyish it made Lyndsay's heart skip, "for somebody with my service record."

Lyndsay cocked an eyebrow. "Another long story?"

"Not really." He took a forkful of beans. "I have a little problem yielding to authority—apparently not a desirable characteristic for a commercial pilot. I never did look all that hot in a uniform anyway."

"So now you fix planes instead of fly them?"

"There's always work for a good mechanic."

But Lyndsay had a feeling there was more to the story than that. A lot more.

They ate in silence for a while, and the glaring white sun dropped lower on the horizon, softening the sky to a dull blue and shadowing the blacktop. The waiter brought another round of beers. Lyndsay found her mind wandering far from the subject of buried treasure and it took a surprising effort to redirect her thoughts.

"So," she said, "how long have you been on the trail of Grandpa Joshua's treasure?"

He smiled. "A few years now."

And men said *women* were enigmatic. She tried a different approach. "You know, not many people have the kind of patience it takes to go after buried treasure. They think once you have a map it's a done deal."

He gave a rueful laugh, expertly picking up his burrito with one hand without spilling any of the contents. "I could sure tell them different."

"Of course," she went on nonchalantly, "a great deal depends on how accurate the map is."

"Naturally."

"But even then, the expense involved, and the time... A lot of people decide it's easier to go for the quick buck and just sell the map to a professional."

He seemed to be a great deal more interested in the burrito he was biting into than in what she was saying. She wondered if she was losing her touch. She did know she wasn't nearly as patient as she once had been. There was a touch of doggedness to her tone as she continued.

"There's a real market for treasure maps, you know."

He still didn't seem very interested, but he did manage a polite, "Oh, yeah?"

"Sure. Investment consortiums, professionals with corporate backing—that's where the real money is in this game."

"You seem to know a lot about it."

She shrugged. "One of the perks of the business."

She pretended to be occupied with spooning a dollop of sour cream atop her enchilada while she commented casually, "A map like yours, for example—assuming it's authentic—might go for as much as ten thousand dollars."

She darted a quick glance at him but could see no discernible change of his expression.

His tone was conversational as he replied, "Ten grand? No kidding. With bucks like that at stake, the treasure-hunting business must be prime hunting ground for scam artists."

That was the last thing she had expected him to say. Moreover, she couldn't help feeling that his eyes hid another message. A warning? A suspicion?

Her annoyance mounted. Just when she was convinced she could read him like a book and play him like a jukebox, he slid into his inscrutable mode and left her baffled and unsure. Jed Donovan had to be the first man she had met in years who had come this close to getting the upper hand with her. Though normally she wouldn't have minded, where money was concerned Lyndsay tended to lose her sense of humor.

She refused to flinch beneath her own mounting frustration. She replied evenly, "Not at all. Treasure hunters—professional ones, that is—have made a lifetime out of telling the fake from the real thing, and they're not all that easily fooled. And of course, some of them are real bad boys, and their backers are even worse. A scam artist might try something, might get away with it, but probably wouldn't enjoy the fruits of his labors much, when all is said and done."

She made up most of that last part, but thought it wouldn't hurt to throw it in just in case.

"Man, this is really starting to sound like big business," Jed murmured.

"Not big business. But business."

Jed had made short work of his Juárez platter—hardly surprising since, Lyndsay realized now, she had done most of the talking. He tossed his napkin on the table, picked up his beer mug and leaned back in his chair, surveying her in an easy relaxed way.

Lyndsay didn't like to be watched while she ate, and there was something particularly unsettling about his quietly observant gaze, but she refused to be intimidated. She was hungry, and there was almost a full plate of food before her. She cut into her enchilada.

"I hate it when people say they like a girl with a healthy appetite," she said. "Just thought I'd warn you."

He smiled. "That wasn't what I was going to say."

She had a feeling she didn't particularly want to hear what he was going to say—nothing that was preceded by a smile that insincere could possibly bode well for her—and she was right.

"I was going to ask," he went on, "what it was like living with a psychic."

Give me a break, Lyndsay thought.

She answered out loud, "You writing a book?"

"Maybe. Maybe I'll tell your story to the tabloids. I ought to get something out of this trip."

Lyndsay put her fork down and touched her napkin to her lips, lifting an eyebrow. "What makes you think you won't get anything out of this trip?"

The smile deepened at one corner, and there was nothing insincere about that look at all. "I meant something tangible."

"So did I."

"Seriously." He didn't look particularly serious. "What was it like? I mean, it must've been pretty hard to sneak anything past him. Did he know who your boyfriends were before you did?"

Lyndsay was starting to become annoyed, and only the suspicion that he was trying to annoy her persuaded her to keep her expression bland and her tone even. "My father's powers—" she almost choked on the word "—were limited to archaeological sites. I would have expected you to know that."

"You'd be surprised how little is known about psychic archaeologists." Still that smile, that maddeningly pleasant tone. "For example, is it something that can be learned, or are you born with it? How do these visions, or whatever you call them, come, anyway? And why do you think your father was a phony?"

Lyndsay stopped in the process of spearing an errant chunk of tomato that had fallen from her taco. She raised her eyes to him slowly.

"Why would you say something like that?" Her voice sounded odd, but considering the dryness of her mouth she was pleased to be able to speak at all.

He drank from the mug, his eyes never straying from her. "A couple of things. When I first came in this afternoon you said, 'Don't tell me you believe in psychics,'—like only a fool would. Then every time you talk about your father you say things like 'a man like that' and describe him as not much of a businessman and just out chasing dreams. I don't think anybody'll ever make the mistake of thinking he was a man you respected."

Lyndsay stiffened, momentarily caught off guard. "That's not fair. It so happens that I love my father very much, and you hardly know me well enough to—"

"Whoa there." He lifted a hand as though to physically restrain her flashing temper. "I never said anything about you not loving your father, just that you didn't much respect him. Or..." Again that too-perceptive look came into his eyes. "Maybe I should say you didn't much respect what he did for a living."

Damn, Lyndsay thought. She *was* losing her touch. She should have known this man was too smart not to read between the lines. Why hadn't she been more careful?

But backtracking was one of her best survival skills. "You're right," she said, injecting just the right note of reluctant contrition into her tone. "I guess I haven't sounded very respectful."

The best lies, as anyone knew, always included part of the truth, and that was what she gave him now. "It's not that I don't believe in my father's powers, it's just that I don't understand them, and that's hard for me to deal with. And you have to understand that my father's—life-style—alienated the entire academic community, which caused me a lot of hardship. I suppose I still resent him for that, and sometimes it shows."

He still looked a little skeptical, but at least not entirely unconvinced. "So how do *you* think he did it?" he wanted to know.

Lyndsay shrugged. "I don't know. I only know that his success rate was over ninety percent."

According to at least one tabloid, she added silently. Lyndsay's private observations of course indicated a success rate that was closer to one percent, and even that, as far as she was concerned, could be explained by normal means.

"Of course," she went on easily, picking up her fork again, "in your case—"

"Let's not talk about my case yet. After all, there's no point in talking about it at all if the good doctor was nothing but a phony, is there?"

With an effort, Lyndsay held on to the frazzled remnants of her patience. "If you thought that, why did you come all this way in the first place? Why did you let me go to all the trouble of searching through my father's notes if you weren't even interested in what he had to say?"

"I'm interested," he assured her. "It's just that right now there are a couple of things that interest me more."

"You remind me of a man trying to out-finagle a used-car salesman."

His chuckle reflected surprise and appreciation. "And you," he returned, "remind me of a used-car salesman."

She frowned. "I don't suppose you meant that as a compliment."

"Actually I did. Where I come from, the most respected man in town is a used-car salesman—probably because he's also the richest."

"Where you come from," she repeated. "And that's—?"

"Three Forks, Oklahoma, population 1750, where that same used-car salesman is not only mayor and head councilman but the most popular camp-meeting preacher in three counties."

Lyndsay grinned. "Sounds like a great place to grow up. Huckleberry Finn material."

"No river."

"You know what I mean. Small town, white picket fences . . ."

"It was okay." He sipped his beer. "I take it you didn't grow up in a small town."

"I grew up in a university—universities," she corrected, finishing off the last of her taco. "Even when he was a regular academic, my father was just enough of an individualist to be unable to stay anyplace long enough to qualify for tenure. A university town is a small town in some ways, though—even if it happens to be Chicago or New York or Los Angeles. Or, I guess I should say it has all the disadvantages and none of the advantages.''

"When did your father stop being a 'regular academic'?'' Jed asked.

At least he was tactful enough not to add, *And decide to be a psychic.*

"My mother died while I was in college. My father took it pretty hard. He went on a sabbatical, and when he returned . . .''

"He had the gift,'' Jed supplied.

She shot him a suspicious look but his expression was unreadable. *Gift.* That was hardly the word she'd use to describe the shock, the despair, the humiliation of watching her once-bright, articulate father deteriorate into a spectacle his contemporaries whispered about and laughed at behind his back. Gift, indeed.

"This town doesn't have much to brag about,'' Lyndsay said, "but there's a spectacular view of the sunset from that little rise behind the motel. Do you want to go for a walk?''

"Sounds fine.''

And it was to Jed's credit that he showed absolutely no surprise at her abrupt change of subject. He paid the bill and reached for his hat, which he settled comfortably on his head again as soon as they were out of the restaurant.

Lyndsay indicated the west side of the parking lot, and the two of them set off together into the desert.

Chapter Five

The worst of the day's heat was gone, but a haze of it still clung to the asphalt and rose up from the desert as they crossed the parking lot. "There's a footpath over there," Lyndsay said, gesturing toward the side of the building.

They left the asphalt and set off across the desert, which was at first littered with crushed cans, scraps of plastic wrap and other debris that had been blown or dragged by night foragers from the nearby dumpster. But within fifty feet or so, those last remnants of civilization disappeared and they were alone with the sand and the evening shadows.

As the path began its slight ascent, the edge of Lyndsay's sandal caught a stone and she stumbled a little. Immediately Jed's hand was on her elbow, strong and supportive. Lyndsay's heart skipped a little—not simply with the surprise of his touch, which was nice, but with a kind of girlish gratification. Men didn't automatically do things like that for

Lyndsay—offer their arms, extend their hands, lend a supporting touch on the back or shoulder—the way they did with smaller, more dainty women. It was not that she needed his support, but she was glad he had offered it.

She was even gladder when, instead of releasing her arm as soon as she regained her footing, his hand slid down the length of her forearm and his fingers entwined with hers. Then her heartbeat *did* skip with pleasure, and she glanced at him, smiling. He smiled back.

Nice, she thought. *Really nice.*

The rise was gentle, but the curvature of the land was such that the sky seemed to fill the entire universe from atop its crest. The sky was indigo, but backlit with a brilliance that cast shadows across the ground so deep, they looked like scars. The clouds were gold and orange and rich, deep rose. But the spectacle paled in comparison to the sensual thrill of standing there close to this lean tall stranger, his strong, rough hand enfolding hers in a surprisingly tender gesture. It was the stuff of which only the best fantasies were made.

"Not bad," he said, indicating the sunset. "But not worth living here for."

"Many's the time I've told myself the exact same thing."

And she turned toward him, stretching out her fingers between his, casting him a smile that was as much of a cross between coy and bold as she could manage. "Of course, it's not every day I get to look at it with a man like you."

The radiating lines at the corners of his eyes deepened. "Don't waste your time flirting with me," he advised. "I'm already convinced."

She was a little taken aback, but that had grown to be such a common feeling where he was concerned that she recovered in less than a beat. She swayed just a fraction closer to him, her fingertips caressing the backs of his knuckles. "Convinced of what?"

He lifted his other hand to her face, and now they were very close. The breath of a breeze fluttered her skirt across his knees, and she could feel the heat of his thighs against hers. His face filled her entire vision.

His fingertip outlined the shape of her lips, which parted automatically, breathlessly, at his touch. Her heart first began to race, then to pound as his finger slipped just inside, caressing the silky inner lining of her upper lip.

"Convinced," he said softly, "that you're a very dangerous woman."

His fingers trailed down, over the shape of her jaw and her chin, lightly stroking her neck. She arched like a cat to his touch, waiting for his kiss, aching for it.

Their entwined hands rested near his leg. Lyndsay stretched her fingers out, caressing the scratchy denim of his jeaned thigh. She tilted her face to his. His breath mingled with hers and she drew it shallowly into her own lungs. His hand moved over her bare shoulder, caressing, exploring. Then he disengaged his other hand from hers and brought both hands up to cup her face. She was dizzy with expectation.

"And that's exactly why I'm not going to kiss you just yet," he said.

It took a moment for the words to penetrate the roaring of anticipation in her ears, and yet another moment for the frantic flare of hormones and tumbling rhythm of her heart to catch up with what she heard.

When she did understand, it was with a jolt. She wanted to fling herself from his arms; she wanted to shout, "What?"; she wanted to turn and march back down the hill in righteous indignation. The reason she did none of those things was because she was entirely too shocked.

He said, "Let's get one thing straight, okay?" His hands remained cupped around her face, but his tone was easy and friendly. "You're a hell of a woman, and a man would have to be dead at least a week not to be turned on by you. But I'm not going to fall into your sex trap, so you may as well stop trying. If you want something from me, you ask me straight out and I'll see what I can do. But I'm not going to play this seduction game of yours, so you may as well stop trying."

Lyndsay looked at him thoughtfully for a long moment, trying not to let him know exactly how disconcerted she was. Her charms had never failed to work on any man before; she had never known a male who could not be manipulated to the ends of the earth with a come-hither smile and a properly presented profile. Was it possible she had finally found a man she could deal with on her own level?

"What if it's not a game?" she asked.

He smiled. "That," he assured her, "is another matter altogether."

He waited, as though giving her a chance to say something else, but Lyndsay didn't know what to say. The truth—that she found him more attractive than any man she had ever met and that her flirtations with him had, from the beginning, been more in earnest than she wanted to admit even to herself— would put her at a definite disadvantage. She was not ready to be honest with this man yet, and she might never be.

He took her silence as a signal and the change of mood between them was palpable.

He dropped his hands from her face. "So," he said in a tone that was perfectly conversational, "tell me what you found."

Lyndsay drew a slow deep breath, and stepped away. "You surprise me."

He smiled. "Because I can resist your charms?"

"Because you do it so well."

"You know what they say. Timing is everything."

He touched her shoulder lightly and indicated the path back down the hill. Lyndsay had no choice but to accept his suggestion as graciously as possible.

One corner of her lips turned down ruefully and she gave a little shake of her head. "You wasted a hell of a sunset." And the trip back down was going to be a great deal less pleasant than the walk up had been.

"But," he said, with a slight admonishing lift of his finger, "the night is yet to come."

Lyndsay glanced up at him and saw the twinkle in his eyes and it took all of her willpower to resist. She was not going to fall for that oh-so-subtle, too-good-to-be-true charm again.

She said, "You know, even my father wouldn't guarantee the accuracy of any of his information. All I have to go on are some notes he made that may or may not even pertain to your case."

"I understand."

She was marginally encouraged. "I'm just guessing here, but it seems to me things must not be going too well in the treasure-hunt game for you to be grasping at straws like this. And that does *not*," she added firmly, "reflect in any way on whether I think my father's information is accurate. You knew it was a long shot when you came here."

"That's right."

He was sinking into his enigmatic mode again. It was maddening.

"If I were in your position," she told him frankly, tired of wasting time, "I'd give serious thought to selling the map, taking a nice profit and being done with it. That's really the only way an amateur is ever going to make any money in this business."

"And I suppose you know just the broker."

She shot him a sharp suspicious look. "I might."

He stopped, and turned toward her. They were reaching the bottom of the incline and he stood, one foot was naturally lower than the other, his knee bent. It was an unconscionably sexy pose, and she wondered if he had chosen it on purpose.

"Just so we don't waste any more time," Jed said, "I'm not in the market to sell my map. I wouldn't even if I wanted to. It's part of my family's history, and as far as I'm concerned it's going to stay in the family. And if I *was* in the market, ten thousand dollars—or even twenty," he added with a deliberate specificity that made Lyndsay feel as though she should blush, "wouldn't even begin to recoup what I've got invested already. So let's just put that subject behind us."

All right, Mr. Hard to Get, Lyndsay thought grimly, *you had your chance, and two can play at that game.* But excitement was rising, and she tried not to let it show on her face. Whether he had meant to or not, he had revealed two important facts—facts which, on the surface, might not seem like much, but to Lyndsay meant the difference between a project worth pursuing, and another man's idle boast.

"I thought you said you drew the map yourself," she said.

Only the slightest trace of a frown shadowed his eyes, and it was gone almost before it registered. "I did."

He started down the hill again.

"But you said it was a part of family history."

"A figure of speech."

Lyndsay had no trouble keeping up with his long strides, though it struck her as amusing that a man who had held her hand on the way up the hill now seemed interested in putting as much distance between them as possible.

"Ten thousand dollars is a lot of money," she mused. "Just exactly how long *have* you been after this treasure?"

The sidelong glance he gave her reflected a great deal more calm than she would have expected. "I don't see what that has to do with what your father may or may not have known about my project."

"You're probably right. But I have a theory."

They were on flat ground now, and twilight painted the desert a dusky blue. The yellow lights of the motel looked farther away than they actually were; nonetheless Lyndsay slowed her step. "Do you want to hear my theory?"

"I have a feeling I'm going to."

"My theory," said Lyndsay, "is that this treasure is a lot more than a weekend hobby to you. You might not be a professional but you're very close to it. I think the map you have is either the original or a copy of the original, not something you just threw together with guesswork. And because of that, and other things I don't know about yet, you're very close to finding that treasure. Just one or two small pieces are missing and those were what you were hoping my father could provide."

Even without the deepening shadows, his face would have been unreadable, and his voice was no more revealing. "So that's your theory."

It was becoming more and more of a struggle to keep the impatience out of her voice. "If you want me to help you, you're going to have to be up-front with me."

"You know what they say—you can't cheat an honest man."

She gave up trying to disguise her impatience. "What's *that* supposed to mean?"

"Just that the people who are most suspicious of others are usually the ones who aren't being entirely up-front themselves."

Lyndsay scowled. The ghost of a headache was beginning to form just between her eyes. Who would have guessed, when Jed Donovan walked into the café that afternoon, that he'd turn out to be this much trouble?

Deliberately she smoothed out her features, and her tone. "My father's journal isn't the easiest thing to decipher under the best of circumstances. It turns out he did make a few entries when he visited Colorado about the time that tabloid article ran."

He shot her a sharp look of surprise when she mentioned Colorado and Lyndsay thought smugly, *Score one.*

She went on. "But you have to understand I can't make any sense of it at all without seeing your map."

"Then let me look at the journal."

"I couldn't do that. There are notes about other things in that journal, some of them quite personal, and it's all mixed together. My father wouldn't want anyone else looking at it, and neither would I."

He murmured, "Hmm." But Lyndsay couldn't tell whether the sound indicated skepticism or understanding.

They had reached the motel, and night was on their heels. Despite the neon sign from the restaurant and the faint glow of porch lights outside each room, the shadows under the eaves were deep. Jed, leading the way, had taken her toward his room, not toward her car. Lyndsay didn't know whether to be insulted by that, or excited.

But as they stepped into the shadows of the walkway Jed turned to her. They both knew a decision had to be made here. She could walk with him to his room, she could turn and cross to the parking lot. He could ask her to stay; he could say good-night.

They stood close together, and the air between them was a thick mixture of intimacy and anticipation, curiosity and restraint. Lyndsay could see Jed's form but not his face. She had no way of knowing what he was going to do or say next.

Therefore, she was not surprised when he said, "What did the diary say?"

She didn't hesitate... much. "There were a lot of jumbled words and phrases, stream of consciousness—that's how it came to him. He was describing a place, but whether it was *your* place..." She let the sentence dangle.

He was stubbornly unresponsive. She hadn't thought it would be that easy. She plunged on. "There were some landmarks. At least I think they're landmarks. They could have been symbols."

"Like what?"

"Well... a tree." She was practically holding her breath now, straining in the dark. Oh, to see his face! "A dead tree, or a killing tree. He referred to it by both terms."

There was a beat of silence, then Jed said softly, "The Widowmaker."

Lyndsay tried not to leap to conclusions. It meant nothing. He could have heard that name somewhere, it didn't mean his map was authentic... but deep inside there was a part of her that was cavorting wildly with joy because she knew it meant *exactly* that. He had the map and it was authentic—what more proof did she need?

Jed's voice was deliberately devoid of expression as he said, "Was that all? A tree?"

"He talked about the fork of a stream."

She could see him nod, thoughtfully, in the dark. "There's one more landmark. Did he say anything about that?"

She was being tested, she could tell that—or rather her father was—just as she herself was testing Jed. She shouldn't have started describing the map, knowing she couldn't finish it, but it was too late to change that now. All she could do was cast caution to the wind.

"There were other things, none of them made sense because of course I can't see what he was describing." Trees, streams, mountains, rivers, bushes...what was left? "There was a rock, or a clump of rocks. Maybe a mountain." Hadn't there been a mountain in the photograph? "Talking Mountain?"

He was very still, and Lyndsay knew she had blown it. Talking Mountain! What had made her say a thing like that? Why hadn't she quit while she was ahead?

And then Jed said, very softly, "Whispering Rock."

Lyndsay went weak with relief. *Whispering Rock.* That must be the third triangulation point! That meant he had the map. The real map. Without a doubt, the map that was worth twenty grand sight unseen, the map that could lead to more riches than her impoverished imagination could even conjure. Her head spun with the import of it all.

For the first time, she heard real urgency in his voice. It was only a hint, but it was definitely there. "Was there anything else?"

Lyndsay looked at him steadily. "Yes. There was a lot more. But, like I said, I really can't tell what applies to you and what doesn't until I see the map."

Her eyes were beginning to adjust to the dark and she could see his face, deeply planed, the gleam of dark eyes. She knew then exactly what the expression "handsome as the devil" meant.

Without warning, his hands slipped out and settled on her hips, urging her close with a gentle pressure. He did not have to urge very hard.

She felt his breath on her face, heard the smile in his voice. "I guess that about covers that subject."

Lyndsay could only explain her confusion by his nearness. How could he keep catching her off guard? *No one* did that.

"Does it?"

"Oh, yeah." His fingers made kneading motions against her hips, gathering and releasing the material of her skirt. "You'd be a fool to tell me any more, and me...well..."

She felt the unexpected dart of his tongue against the corner of her lips. She shivered with the sensation.

His voice was low and husky and rich with sensuality. "The thing is, darlin', I don't show my treasure map to anybody...not on a first date, anyway."

Lyndsay settled her hands against the back of his neck, her face tilted upward to better drink him in. "What do you do on a first date?"

"Well, now, that's not easy to say in just a few words. But it's always hot and wet and deep, and if we play our cards right, it can last all the way into the tomorrow. And it usually starts something like this." His mouth covered hers.

It was, without a doubt, the best kiss Lyndsay had ever had. And it wasn't so much a kiss as it was an inhaling, a blending, a flaming of skins and a melting of breaths, the quick hot frantic mating of tongues, the long slow deep merger of sensual exploration. Her fingertips went numb. Fever left her weak and robbed her muscles of strength. He kissed her and desire blossomed between her legs, closed up her throat, flared through every nerve ending.

His hands cupped her buttocks and tightened there, pushing her against his hardness. She pressed herself into him, drawing his mouth down to hers with her hands hard on the back of his neck. Her breasts were crushed against his chest, swollen nipples aching with the heat and the strength of him. His mouth left hers and traveled over her face, breath and touch and hot moist sweep of his tongue exploring the contours of her lips and her jaw and her neck. She tasted the roughness of his cheek and the fullness of his lips. She could not recall ever having been plunged this close to the edge of control so quickly before, not by any man.

Her hands pressed downward, over his shoulders and the strong line of his back, resting against the barrier of his leather belt as she forced herself to turn her face away from his, dragging in breaths. "You know," she said with difficulty, "it's a shame."

He drew in a deep breath against the skin of her neck and a flare of nerve endings responded, echoing sensation all the way down her spine. He said, "About what?"

Lyndsay fought against the need to let her eyes drift closed and her hands, her mouth—indeed, her entire body—do what they would. "That you don't want to play the game."

His hands slid down the outside of her arms, caressing her fingers, then releasing her. He was still close enough to permeate the very air she breathed with his scent and the promise of closeness, yet they no longer touched.

"There are a lot of games I enjoy playing," he said softly, "but when it comes to men and women, I'm dead serious. The stakes are too high."

Lyndsay drew in a slightly unsteady breath. "Then what was that kiss about?"

He smiled. "Just to show you what you're missing."

"I see."

She regarded him steadily while her heartbeat calmed and her temperature tried to seek a normal level. Could she believe anything he said? Why did she even want to? One thing was certain—playing any kind of game with him would be the most dangerous thing she had ever done.

An anticipatory shiver raced down her spine.

She said quietly, "You're the most exciting man I've ever met."

"Thank you. The feeling is mutual."

"And also the most confusing."

"Also mutual."

"We really have a lot in common," she went on, pressing her luck. "I think we'd make a good team."

"It's a little early to be talking marriage, isn't it?"

Lyndsay tilted her head back to look at him. His eyes were like jewels in the darkness, full of hidden lights.

"That's not the kind of partnership I had in mind."

"I see." He reached out and combed his fingers through her hair, lifting a strand and letting it fall. "And those things we have in common..."

"Well..." She drew a long, steadying breath as his fingers drifted away from her hair. "You have the treasure map. My father's notebook could be the key that unlocks the chest, so to speak. Put them together and..."

He finished her sentence. "Wealth beyond your wildest dreams."

"Right."

"Of course, how do I know this diary of yours is any good?"

"How do I know your map is any good?"

"You should let me look at the diary."

"You should let me see the map."

He chuckled, his eyes dancing with subtle lights that set off a network of reciprocal sparks inside Lyndsay.

"You're right," he said. "We do have a lot in common. But there's just one thing. I didn't bring the map with me."

Lyndsay's smile didn't fade. "I didn't imagine you had."

"Good. I'd hate for you to be disappointed."

He moved as though to draw her close again. Lyndsay lifted her hands to his shoulders with a gentle restraint. "No games, remember?"

"Who said I was playing?"

Lyndsay's heartbeat speeded, and it was all she could do to step away. "Think about what I said," she suggested. "We need each other."

He didn't reply, and she turned toward the parking lot. "Good night, Donovan."

His thoughtful gaze followed her as she walked away. After a moment he murmured, "Maybe we do at that."

Lyndsay heard him, and her pulse leapt with hope. But she didn't turn around.

Chapter Six

Jed dragged one of the wooden chairs from his room out the door and sat there thinking, watching the stars and appreciating the cool night air after the heat of the day.

He did not expect to be able to sleep. He hated motel rooms, for one thing, and never got a good night's sleep in them. For another thing, after the treatment she'd given him, a man would have to be less than human to just forget about it and drop off to sleep.

He grinned a little, remembering. Not that he hadn't deserved it. Not that he hadn't enjoyed every minute of it. And not, of course, that he intended to let her get away with it.

Sometimes life was good.

He half expected her to come back, but he knew that was mostly wishful thinking. That would be too easy, too predictable. And the one thing Lyndsay Blake was not, was predictable. What bothered him was how much he wanted her to come back, how hard it had been to just let her walk away tonight.

But he had told her the truth when he said he didn't play games with women—particularly with a woman like her—because doing so was far too dangerous.

He could not remember a time when he hadn't been focused on the treasure—researching it, studying it, dreaming about it, looking for it. Lyndsay was right—this was more than a weekend hobby. It was very nearly an obsession, and, as a rule, obsessed men did not have much energy left over for anything else. Jed's relationships with women had of necessity been short-lived, but he had never taken them lightly.

Never had he met a woman who excited him, challenged him, perplexed him and intrigued him as much as Lyndsay Blake did, and he took her very seriously indeed. Since he had met her, he had spent almost as much time thinking about her as he had about the treasure, and that was disturbing—because she could threaten not only his peace of mind, but also the one thing he had spent his entire life seeking.

More than once tonight she had referred to professional treasure hunters, and by strictest definition Jed was not one of them. A professional would have never spent as much time and effort—not to mention money—on a single enterprise with such dismal hope of a payoff. A professional would have calculated the odds, made a reasonable investment and walked away long before now. But to a professional, the treasure was just a means to an end— something to be traded for money, which would in turn be invested in another treasure hunt and turned into more money.

To Jed, the treasure was a way of life, his heritage. It was money, yes, but the money to him meant freedom—his own airplane, a chance to fly again, to live his life the way he wanted and seek out his own pleasures and satisfactions. More importantly, it meant the fulfillment of a quest passed down to him from his father, and his father before him. The treasure was his to find and he intended to find it. In that sense, he supposed he was obsessed.

He kept trying to figure out how Lyndsay knew about the map. It was possible, he supposed, that she could have heard about the Widowmaker and the stream. But the third triangulation point, Whispering Rock...that wasn't even on the map. His grandfather had called it Whispering Rock, and as far as Jed knew he was the last person to use that phrase.

Then how had she known?

Or perhaps he should ask how her father had known. Because it was beginning to look as though the old archaeologist had had a lot more going for him than the supermarket rags had indicated.

He leaned back, balancing the chair on its two rear legs, resting his shoulders against the wall. The sky was littered with stars, brilliant with them, and out here in the desert, away from the city lights, the panorama seemed to go on forever. At moments like this it was easy to understand the reluctance his ancestors had felt about sleeping under a roof. At moments like this he wanted to be in the air, alone with the night and the purr of an engine, so badly he could taste it.

It was possible, Jed supposed, that records of the treasure existed beyond the one he had. Unlikely, but possible. It was even possible that the old man had stumbled upon some of them in his research about the area. And it was beginning to look more and more possible that he might actually have discovered the exact spot where the money was hidden. Or had at least come closer to it than Jed ever had.

One thing was for sure. He had neither reproduced the map nor left very clear instructions about how to reach the site. If he had, that daughter of his would have been out of here so fast, it would make his head spin.

No, more than likely she was telling the truth when she said she needed the map to interpret the diary—just as he needed the diary to interpret the map. The information she had was apparently not enough. But just what *did* she have? That was what Jed needed to know.

He had to get his hands on that diary. And if he had to go through Ms. Lyndsay Blake to do it, well...

He smiled to himself in the dark, pulled his hat brim down low on his forehead and closed his eyes peacefully. Sometimes life was, indeed, good.

"I THOUGHT I'd find you up here."

Lyndsay jumped a little at the sound of the male voice. For one absurd moment she had thought it was . . . well, someone else.

She smiled and gestured Duke over. "Come on over. The view's great."

She was sitting on the roof wall, her legs swinging over the side, the sky surrounding her, the desert below her. Facing away from the highway, there were no lights to mar the landscape, and the stars were so close they were almost three-dimensional. It was like being suspended in midair.

Duke sat beside her, but in profile, choosing to keep his feet on the flat firm surface of the roof. "Short date, wasn't it?"

"It served my purpose."

Duke winced. "Now why does that make me feel like I should send the poor guy a sympathy card?"

A gentle gust of breeze combed through Lyndsay's hair and she tilted her head back to better enjoy it. The sensation reminded her of Jed's fingers.

"You men," she scoffed lazily, "you're all alike. You keep saying you want a woman who's your equal, but the minute you get one . . ."

"Excuse me?" Duke lifted a finger in mild protest. "I don't believe I ever said I wanted an equal. In fact I'm sure of it."

Lyndsay grinned at him in the dark. "That's right, I forgot. You want a love slave."

"Or a mother. Either one will do. So how about your cowboy? What does he want?"

Lyndsay smiled to herself, bracing her hands on either side of her on the wall and swinging her feet free. "Me, for one."

Duke slapped his forehead in mock surprise. "You don't mean it!"

"The only question is, how bad?"

"If the fate of the free world were riding on that one, sport, I'd be betting on you."

"I appreciate that vote of confidence, but right now I'm not particularly interested in the fate of the free world. It's my own freedom that I'm thinking about."

A note of sobriety crept into Duke's voice. "Yeah. I figured."

Lyndsay glanced at him with a smile that was half apologetic, half sympathetic. For a while neither of them spoke.

Then Lyndsay said softly, "That sky looks like it goes on forever, doesn't it?"

"Or at least to Oklahoma."

"Colorado," Lyndsay said. "The dig is in Colorado."

Duke nodded.

After a moment he said, "Do you know how long it's been?"

"Two years."

He gave a little shake of his head. "I never figured you'd be here that long."

"Me, either."

His tone was quiet and thoughtful. "You were pretty bruised up when your dad died, a lot more than you realized I think. I knew it'd take you awhile to get yourself together, and this was as good a place as any to do it in."

After two years, Lyndsay, too, could finally look back and understand the enormity of the grief that had paralyzed her, the lack of purpose that had drifted over her and robbed her of will until she could have drowned in her own helplessness. All her life she had taken care of her father—resenting him, loving him, despairing over him, even hating him sometimes, but always a part of him. Then suddenly he was gone and she was lost.

"I was just so used to him, you know?" she agreed softly. It still hurt, sometimes, to talk about him. "To taking care of him, to worrying about him. And then he wasn't there, and it was like I didn't know what to do with myself."

"Sure. Understandable. It was a habit as much as anything else, you and your dad. Lately, though, I was beginning to wonder if hiding out here wasn't getting to be a habit, too."

Lyndsay cast him a sharp glance, but he said nothing else. After a moment her shoulders slumped, and she admitted, "Yeah, I guess you're right. It was getting to be a habit, doing nothing."

"It's still easier than doing something," he pointed out, and then smiled. "Believe me, I know. I've been here fifteen years."

Again they sat in silence, comfortable. She felt safe here, Lyndsay realized. Here nothing happened, here nothing challenged her... here no one would ever make her care and then abandon her. Here her heart was safe.

Or at least it had been, until Jed Donovan sauntered into the café that afternoon and turned the world upside down. Suddenly she wanted again, and she knew she would never be safe again.

At length, Lyndsay said, "Of course I've thought about teaching. Not a prestigious university job, I know that's out, but this country's filled with small colleges who'd kill to have someone with my education and never even notice who my father is."

"So true."

"Or I could sign on as some smart-ass professor's assistant. God, I'd hate being anybody's assistant. But it would be the work I love and a chance to travel...."

"It's a living."

She was silent for a time longer, swinging her feet, gazing at the stars. Then she said softly, "How many times in a person's life does the chance come along for a real adventure?''

Duke said gently, "When are you leaving?"

Lyndsay turned to him, and smiled. He opened his arms and she embraced him, long and hard, squeezing her eyes tightly closed. "You've been a good friend, Duke."

"Yeah, well..." His voice sounded thick. "I want you to know the only reason I never made a pass at you is because you scare the hell out of me."

She leaned back a little to look at him. "Afraid I'd say no?"

"Afraid you'd say yes."

Lyndsay laughed, moving out of the embrace but holding on to his hand in a comfortable companionable manner as they watched the stars together for another few moments.

Then Duke said, "I guess I should ask what you're going to do to the poor sap."

"Nothing that's not for his own good."

"Many a poor sailor has met his fate with *that* siren's song."

"I wouldn't waste any sympathy on Jed Donovan if I were you. I've got a feeling he can take care of himself."

"Then maybe I should worry about you."

"Hardly."

"He's just another dreamer, Lyns," Duke said quietly. "And you know he's going to break your heart."

Lyndsay felt a chill of uneasiness run up her spine, and she avoided Duke's eyes. "My heart's cast-iron shielded by now, Duke. Besides," she added with slightly more conviction, "he's not going to get a chance. He's just a means to an end for me."

Duke gave a sad little shake of his head. "You sure know how to pick 'em, Lyns. First that old boy-friend of yours, and your dad, then me..."

"Don't sell yourself short. You're not even in the same class."

"Now this slick-talking treasure hunter. You must really have a thing for hard-luck cases. Or maybe you're just a glutton for punishment."

"Or maybe, I'm due for a change of luck."

But when she met his eyes, she did not see any encouragement there. He said quietly, "You just be careful, okay?"

Lyndsay swung her feet back onto the roof. "You'd do better to wish me luck. That I'm going to need."

"Then good luck. And be careful."

But Lyndsay just smiled. She had a feeling she'd already passed the point of being careful, and she knew better than anyone that luck, in a game like this, was not a factor.

JED WALKED AROUND to the bed of his pickup the next morning and came face-to-face—in a manner of speaking—with one of the shapeliest backsides he had seen in a long time. He spent a few moments just admiring it.

He had a feeling Lyndsay knew he was there at least thirty seconds before she turned around. His feeling was confirmed by the slightly challenging lift of her eyebrow when she glanced over her shoulder at him, by the deliberate little wiggle she gave her bottom as she leaned forward to make sure her duffel bag was secure against the back of the cab. Jed grinned in sheer delight.

He pushed back his hat and deepened his drawl as she turned around. "Morning, ma'am. Going somewhere, are you?"

Lyndsay stood up, brushing the dust off her knees. "That depends." She squinted up at the sun. "If we don't get started pretty soon we might as well call the whole thing off and try again tomorrow."

Jed was amazed by the fact that the same woman could look equally as provocative in a waitress uniform, a sexy off-the-shoulder dress, and the practical desert garb she wore today. Was it possible, he wondered, for her to look bad?

The khaki shorts she wore stopped just above her knees and were designed more for function than fashion; with them she wore sturdy hiking boots and white socks, and a long-sleeved white cotton shirt unbuttoned over a plain tan T-shirt. Her hair was pulled back in a ponytail at the nape of her neck and topped with a wide-brimmed hat. There was nothing revealing or alluring about her apparel at all, but just looking at her made Jed's mouth water.

He tossed his own bag into the back of the truck and said, "Mind telling me what you're doing in the back of my truck?"

She threw one leg over the side panel, then the other, and jumped to the ground before Jed could even offer to help her. She said briskly, "I should think that would be obvious. I'm going with you."

"Are you now? Mother will be delighted."

She scowled briefly at him. "Come on, Donovan, that's no way to treat someone who's doing you a favor."

He leaned his elbow against the top of the side panel, surveying her at leisure. "No, I reckon it's not. What kind of favor are you doing me, if you don't mind me asking?"

"I'm going to help you find that gold."

The grin that had been lurking on his lips deepened. "Why, that's right generous of you."

"Generous has nothing to do with it, as you know very well. We're partners or nothing at all."

"I don't need a partner."

"You need something. If you didn't, you wouldn't have come to my father for help."

"Yeah, well he had something I needed."

She looked him square in the eye. "So do I."

He rubbed one knuckle against the side of his jaw ruefully, and let his eyes sweep over her figure in undisguised appreciation. "I'm not denying that. But what he had might have helped me find the treasure.''

She poked her index finger into his chest, hard. There was no amusement in her face whatsoever. ''Now you see there, Donovan, that's what you get for thinking with your hormones. If you'd just spend a few minutes using that part of your brain that's above the waist it might have occurred to you that I could have a function in life *besides* contributing to your sexual fantasies.''

''Sweetheart, that might be. But when I'm with you, I'm not even sure I have anything above the waist.''

She looked at him fiercely for another moment, and then slowly she grinned. With a slight shove for emphasis she removed her finger from his chest. ''Just as long as we know where we stand.''

''Absolutely no doubt about that,'' he assured her soberly, and her grin widened even as she tried to disguise it by turning away.

Women, he thought, amused. Last night as seductive as a geisha, this morning as businesslike as a drill sergeant, with no apology or explanation for either behavior... and he found her equally as fascinating in either mode.

''So what is it,'' he asked, ''that you have to offer besides sexual fantasies—and a diary that may or may not be worth the paper it's written on?''

''I'm an archaeologist, for one thing. That means I've forgotten more about digging up lost treasures than you'll ever know. I know how to dig, when to dig, what to look for—and, to an extent, where to look. If you'd hired a professional in the first place, you could have cut your search time in half."

For some reason, that surprised Jed—but then again, everything about her was a constant surprise to him. There was no reason in the world she shouldn't have followed her father's academic calling and studied archaeology—just as there was no reason in the world for a qualified archaeologist to be working as a waitress in a roadside diner in the middle of nowhere.

"I'm looking for a chest full of gold," he said, "not a lost Indian tribe, you know. It's not going to take a whole lot of skill for me to recognize it when I find it, and I really don't need anybody to brush the dust off the lid and make sure I don't damage the lock when I bust it open. I don't see what good an archaeologist is going to do me at all, and I'm sure as hell not going to take on a partner for those qualifications."

She gave him a scornful glance. "Your ignorance has just proven exactly how much you need me."

She started to move past him toward the cab, but he shifted his position slightly, blocking her way. She didn't back off and neither did he and they stood chest-to-chest and nose-to-nose, a position that Jed found perfectly agreeable.

"Let me just make one thing clear," he said. "I might want you from time to time, maybe even a lot of the time. But I don't need anybody."

Her smile was faint and easy and completely unfazed. "Good for you, cowboy," she said. "I always did like a challenge."

But when she was standing that close to him, hypnotizing him with her eyes and suffusing him in the intoxicating perfume that was the simple essence of her, Jed thought she might not find him as much of a challenge as she imagined.

He held his ground, and so did she.

"I've spent a lifetime tracking down this site," he said. "You said yourself there are people who'd pay hard cash for my map. And I'm supposed to just take you there, give it all away, just because you decide you want to go?"

She spared him a superficial smile. "Give me a little credit, Donovan. You and I both know that without the map one piece of ground looks just like the other. And without the diary, apparently, even the map is worthless."

"Not entirely worthless," he murmured.

She looked at him sharply.

"You have it with you?"

"The diary? Of course."

"What if I offer to buy it off you?"

"Sure. The asking price is one and a quarter million."

He tipped his hat back, gazing toward the highway. "Just as well. My daddy raised me to know better than to buy a pig in a poke, and for all I know that diary of yours is nothing but a bunch of hen scratchings and crayon drawings."

She just smiled. "So what's it going to be, Donovan? One hundred percent of nothing, or fifty percent of two and a half million?"

He appeared to think about that for a minute. "Eighty percent," he said.

"Forty."

"Seventy."

"Thirty."

He grinned. "You are something else, aren't you, little lady?"

"So I've been told. And I've also been known to leave permanent disfiguring scars on men who call me 'little lady.'"

"I don't doubt that a bit."

He stood there looking at her for a time, relishing the feel of the sun on his shoulders and a future that had never looked better. He said, "You know, it'd almost be worth having you along just to brighten up the scenery."

"Worth fifty percent?"

"For a million and a quarter, I can live with the scenery I've got."

He turned toward the cab. "I'll tell you what, though. You let me have a look at that diary and we'll negotiate."

She didn't budge. "You heard my deal. Take it or leave it."

He turned back, gazing at her thoughtfully. "You sound mighty confident."

"Take me with you and I guarantee you neither one of us will walk away from this thing broke."

Jed knew, of course, that only a fool would take her promises at face value, and only a crazy man would risk everything on this stranger. But he had already done the craziest thing, by seeking out her father. And hadn't he been prepared to take the professor back to the site, if that was what it took? No one could be as insistent as she was unless she had an ace in the hole somewhere, and it certainly behooved him to find out just what it was she had in mind.

But the truth was, of course, he had never had any intention of leaving this place without her. He had made up his mind about that last night.

He said, "I haven't had breakfast."

She opened the passenger door. "We'll stop on the way."

She got in and slammed the door. Jed couldn't stop a self-congratulatory grin as he moved around to the driver's door; fortunately she didn't see. He settled his hat on his head at a slightly more rakish angle than before, and was whistling a little tune under his breath as he dug in his pocket for his keys.

Who would've thought it would be this easy?

Chapter Seven

Who would've thought it would be this easy? Lyndsay observed a little dazedly once they were well down the highway and she could relax. *Whoever would have thought?*

She had done it. She had packed everything she owned into a single duffel bag, climbed into a stranger's pickup and was on her way to track down buried treasure.

Well, not exactly, she amended, but she was tracking down a treasure map, which was almost as exciting and a lot closer to a sure thing as far as it went. But even if it all proved to be nothing but smoke and dust it had gotten her out of that dust hole in which she had almost convinced herself she would die. And for that alone it was worth it.

Lyndsay comfortably slid lower in the seat, propping one foot up on the dashboard and sliding a covert glance toward her companion beneath the pulled-down brim of her hat. Just looking at him made her heart speed up with excitement. The strong square profile of his shadowed jaw, the curl of hair that lay against his neck, the shape of the muscle beneath the sleeve of his T-shirt, the way his hand controlled the wheel of the truck with the same ease with which he had caressed her last night... Lyndsay's stomach tightened in a kind of delighted yearning with the memory.

She could hardly believe it. She had actually run away with this man.

And the adventure had only begun.

She spent a few moments savoring that possibility, and when she was fairly sure she could look at him without giving away every thought in her head she said, "Tell me about the eyewitness."

Again he darted her an amused glance. "You're really all business, aren't you?"

"Is there something else I should be?"

"Well, I seem to recall yesterday you weren't quite so single-minded."

"Wasn't I?" She lifted an eyebrow. "Beware the wiles of a scheming woman."

His eyes left the road long enough to travel up the length of the leg that was propped on the dashboard, from the cuffs of the socks to the cuffs of the shorts. "Or man," he murmured.

Lyndsay chuckled. "Scheming, maybe. Wiles..." She looked him over frankly. "Somehow that's not a word that leaps to mind when I think of you. It implies a certain subtlety that just doesn't quite seem in character."

"Oh, yeah? I don't think I like that."

He was thoughtful for a moment. "So what words do leap to mind when you think of me?"

Lyndsay grinned. "Oh, the insatiable male ego. You're just not comfortable in any conversation that doesn't revolve around you."

He shared her grin. "That's what makes us perfect together, hon. I want to talk about me, you hate to talk about you. So you were saying?"

Lyndsay settled back against the seat again, choosing her words. "Determined," she decided in a moment. "That's a word that leaps to mind. And stubborn. Sharp as a riverboat gambler—"

He chuckled.

"—and just about as honest."

"Hey," he objected mildly.

She gave him a measuring look. "And of course, sexy."

"*That's* the word I was looking for."

"And that's the one thing that's completely irrelevant."

"Is it, now?"

"Or," she amended, "I probably should say it's the one thing about you that *doesn't* worry me. Sexy men are a dime a dozen."

He pretended to consider that. "I probably should be insulted, but I kind of like the idea I worry you."

"*Worry* is probably too strong a word. But it's good for me to be a little concerned, it keeps me alert."

"And I like my women alert," agreed Jed soberly.

Lyndsay grinned. "Tell me about the eyewitness, Donovan."

She saw one corner of his lips tighten in a conciliatory smile, but he didn't take his eyes off the highway. The brim of his hat cast a sharp shadow across the upper half of his face, adding a touch of drama to his appearance that Lyndsay couldn't help admiring.

He settled back to tell the story.

"In 1870," he said, "Colorado mostly belonged to the outlaws and the ranchers, and even those were few and far between. Now, it takes a lot of Colorado land to feed a cow, so the ranches we're talking about are pretty good-sized spreads. By the time Joshua passed through, there weren't too many places you could go without being on somebody's land—except for this one parcel out near the Four Corners region. Legend said it was Indian holy ground."

He glanced at her to ascertain her reaction, and Lyndsay obliged him by rolling her eyes. "Nice touch."

"You wanted a story."

"Did I forget to mention I'd like to have it as close to the truth as possible?"

"Actually, that is the truth." Again a glance in her direction. "I'm surprised your father didn't mention it. In his notes, I mean."

Lyndsay frowned a little, absently. "So am I," she murmured, and what she meant was she was surprised *Jeffrey* hadn't mentioned it. She added quickly, "Or maybe he did and I just didn't recognize it."

"It'd be pretty hard to miss a detail like that."

Lyndsay kept her voice cool. "Not really. Maybe my father didn't consider it particularly relevant."

"Hmm," he agreed, deadpan. "Could be. Indian holy ground is a dime a dozen around these parts."

She glanced at him suspiciously but his face revealed nothing.

She prompted impatiently, "What does this have to do with—"

"I'm getting there," he assured her. "The fact is, my theory has always been that Joshua *deliberately* headed for this holy ground, knowing the local ranchers were spooked by it and no self-respecting thief would be poking around there—or hell, maybe he believed the legends himself and thought the spirits of the Old Ones would protect his treasure—"

"What legends?" Lyndsay interrupted, curious now.

He ignored her. "At any rate, he certainly would have known about it, and if you trace his route back from Denver, you'll see there would have been quite a few faster ways to get home. He probably knew he was being followed—or knew he would be—and had already picked out his hiding place.''

Lyndsay was beginning to follow his logic. She listened intently.

"What he didn't know—and couldn't have stopped if he did—was that a young cowpoke would be out scouting strays and see the whole thing as Joshua came riding into the hollow, the three bandits hot on his trail. Now the cowboy—Rafe, was his name—he was only fourteen years old at the time and nobody's hero. He was curious enough to watch but not curious enough to cross over onto the holy ground—or haunted ground, as they called it back then—to get a better look, so Joshua, as he was scrambling to hide the gold, passed in and out of his line of sight. When the lead started to fly, Rafe hightailed it back to the ranch, but to his credit, he did bring back help. Of course, it was too late by then.

"Later, he heard about the gold and he got over his superstitions about the holy ground right quick. He looked for it. According to reports, he spent the best part of his young manhood looking for it. But you've got to remember he never actually *saw* where Joshua hid the gold. He only saw the general direction. And he took his failure to mean the place *was* cursed I guess, or else he got sentimental in his old age. Because fifty years later he looked up my grandfather, to whom he figured the gold rightfully belonged, and—"

"Gave him the map," Lyndsay said softly.

Not a muscle in Jed's face moved and he finished as smoothly as though he hadn't heard a word, "—told him the story."

"That's it, isn't it?" Lyndsay insisted, her excitement rising. "He didn't find the gold but he found the map. If Joshua knew in advance where he was going to hide the gold, he had time to make a map— or hell, maybe somebody made the map for *him* to show him where the hiding place was. And it *was* hidden, not buried—he didn't have time to bury it, am I right? Sure it all falls into place. The only thing I don't understand is if the cowboy had the map all the time, why he didn't find the gold."

Jed said mildly, "You're sure you're not psychic?"

Lyndsay raised her other foot to the dashboard and crossed her ankles, folding her arms over her chest triumphantly. "So I'm right. Joshua drew the map and—" she shot him a challenging look "—you have it."

Jed's eyes remained on the flat unchanging surface of the road, and his expression was equally unrevealing.

"Rafe took the map off Joshua's body when they were preparing him for burial," he said. "The thing was, he didn't know what he had, all those years. It was written in Creek, you see, and he thought the

drawings were some kind of hieroglyphics, I guess.
But he kept it all those years, and when his conscience finally got the best of him he turned it over
to Joshua's family, as kind of an apology for keeping the secret about the gold for so long."

"Amazing," murmured Lyndsay.

Jed nodded. "He had the key all the time. If he'd
ever once guessed what he had we'd both be out of
work today."

"But he didn't?" Lyndsay's voice was sharp with
suspicion. To come this close...

Jed shook his head. "All he had to his name was
a two-room house and a five-hundred-dollar insurance policy when he died."

"And a map worth two and a half million dollars." Lyndsay practically breathed the words.

Jed raised an eyebrow. "I thought you said it was
worth ten thousand."

She looked at him. "Why did you tell me all this?"

He just smiled. "Partners, remember?"

Lyndsay thought that anyone who was taken in by
a smile that innocent deserved what she got. But the
smile was still a great deal harder to resist than it
should have been.

She said, "Not to mention the fact that I would
have uncovered the story sooner or later anyway."

"If you're half the archaeologist you claim to be
you would have."

"This is not a competition, you know." Lyndsay
abandoned her bantering tone. "If we're going to

work together we really ought to start out by trusting each other."

"You just hit on the number-one reason I never wanted a partner," Jed said.

He glanced at her and his expression was completely serious, his tone matter-of-fact despite the words—which could have been interpreted as a veiled threat.

"There might be one or two people in this world I trust," he said, "and that's only because I know their limits. You're not one of them."

Lyndsay nodded. "Because you don't know my limits."

Jed corrected mildly, "Because I do."

Lyndsay knew she should argue with that for the sake of appearances at least, but she couldn't think of a single thing to say. Wasn't that more or less the same way she felt about him?

Only she wasn't at all sure she knew his limits.

Staring out the window, she said, "Sounds like a pretty cynical philosophy to me."

"Maybe. But I find it keeps people happier all the way around. Nobody expects anything, nobody's disappointed. Life runs a whole lot smoother if you learn not to depend on anybody but yourself."

Lyndsay cast a sharp glance at him, for one disoriented moment suspecting him of taunting her with her own words, as Duke was fond of doing. But Jed had never heard her say that and didn't know her well enough to guess how often she had done so.

It was unsettling, to hear her own words echoed back to her by a virtual stranger. She had never realized how lonely and . . . well, bitter, they sounded.

Their route had so far taken them through familiar and uncompelling territory—the Navajo reservation to the south, the Ute reservation to the west, barren mesa and tumbled red cliff everywhere. Now as Jed made a right turn onto a state road at a sign that pointed toward Titusville, Merrimack and Sinbad, Lyndsay took the opportunity to change the subject.

"So what were you doing in Oklahoma if the dig is in Colorado?"

Jed seemed to relax at the neutral turn of the conversation.

"Working," he answered. "Most of my contacts are back there, and when I can't get a job closer to the site, that's where I go."

He cast her a rueful look. "This time of year I'm usually based in Colorado, though, and that's why it threw me for a minute yesterday when you made that comment about driving all the way from Oklahoma."

Lyndsay's attention was on a passing road sign as she made a mental map of their route—just in case. She murmured, "That's what you get for using your mother's address to register your car."

He gave her an odd look, but only replied, "A man's got to have his mail sent somewhere."

Twenty minutes later they reached Titusville, a flat, undistinguished little town not so different from the one she'd escaped. There was a gas station, a laundry, a couple of eating establishments and a twelve-unit motel that advertised free cable and a great view of the mountains. Some people might have called the rugged San Juan range, tan and red in the far distance, beautiful, but Lyndsay preferred cable.

Jed pulled up in front of a small grocery store. "I hope you brought cash. I only planned on provisioning for one."

Lyndsay gave him a dry look as she got out of the truck.

The wooden building looked deceptively small from the outside; inside its narrow aisles were crowded with foodstuffs and sundries of every description. Jed took a basket and began to methodically toss in canned goods and boxes of cereal and crackers. Lyndsay grimaced when he added powdered milk, and cheered a little when he tossed in a variety pack of cookies.

"No refrigerator, huh?" she said.

"I don't have time to be running back and forth to town for fresh milk. I stay until I use up all the supplies, then take a day and restock."

The way the basket was beginning to fill up, it looked as though he wouldn't be restocking for a month or two. Lyndsay began to add a few supplies of her own.

"So what do we cook on, a camp stove?" She studied the package directions on what appeared to be some kind of artificially preserved lasagna dinner.

"Microwave."

Lyndsay lifted an eyebrow, more than a little curious now to see his camp. After a moment's debate, she tossed the lasagna into the basket.

Jed added five pounds of coffee and a case of beer, then, to her surprise, went to the frozen-foods section and practically emptied the case of TV dinners.

"No refrigerator, but a freezer?"

"I didn't say I didn't have a refrigerator," he replied. "I just said I didn't waste it on fresh milk. How do you think I keep the beer cool?"

"Of course." Lyndsay added potato chips, peanut butter and all the licorice on the counter display. Jed shot her an amused look but said nothing.

They split the bill and loaded the boxes of supplies in the back of the truck.

Lyndsay knew they were close to their destination for no other reason than the tension she could feel from Jed the moment he started the truck again. Though his expression remained relaxed, excitement seemed to radiate from him in waves, and it was contagious. They spoke little for the remainder of the trip.

This part of the country had changed little over the past hundred years, and still looked much the same as it must have looked to Joshua on his last fateful trip. The air was brilliantly clear, almost painful to the eyes at times, for the elevation was high enough to escape the pollutants, natural and man-made, of the valleys below. It was rugged country, almost monochromatic with its shades of red and brown and gray-white tumbled boulders, stark and isolated.

Lyndsay knew this land well, both from her own studies and from her explorations with her father. The Four Corners area—so called because the common border shared by Utah, Arizona, Colorado and New Mexico was the only place in the United States where four states met—had been a particular interest of her father's for most of his life, and one she'd eventually come to share.

Not far were the famous Pueblo Cliff Dwellings, where Lyndsay had spent a great deal of her time as a young college student. To the east was Mesa Verde National Park. Most of the remaining countryside was reservation land, but there were strips of green farmland along the riverbeds, and big ranches in the north, just as it had been in Joshua's time. It made Lyndsay feel a little odd to realize how much time both she and her father had spent studying this area, not realizing that the biggest find of the century was right under their noses.

Jed made a turn off the state road onto a narrow, one-lane blacktop, and another turn onto a dirt road and finally he left the road altogether. As the truck's less-than-perfect shocks bounced and swayed over the rubble-littered track, Lyndsay began to understand why Joshua had needed a map to find this place.

The track began to narrow between two towering boulders, and abruptly ended at a guardhouse and a chain-link fence. The locked gate bore a sign clearly lettered in red: Danger! Do Not Enter! And in smaller black letters: U.S. Government Research Station. Below that was the yellow warning sign for radioactivity.

Jed put the truck in Park, calmly got out and unlocked the gate. Lyndsay watched, stupefied, expecting machine-gun fire to open up from the guardhouse at any moment.

Jed pushed the gate open and returned to the truck. Lyndsay was unable to find her voice until he had driven the truck through and relocked the gate.

"My God. Don't tell me you're poaching on government land."

He grinned at her. "Getting cold feet?"

"And not just government land—a nuclear-testing center! And I thought *I* was desperate!"

He laughed as he put the truck in gear and they started off once again across the grassy rock-strewn ground. "While I kind of like being thought of as intrepid, I guess I have to tell the truth. I put the gate up."

She stared at him. "And the signs?"

"Those I stole."

"But the guardhouse—"

"Nothing but plywood facade."

Lyndsay sank back against the seat, still staring. "For heaven's sake, *why?*" She made a terse gesture toward their surroundings. "It's not as though this place is on every tourist's map. Don't you think the whole thing's just a little bit paranoid?"

He shrugged. "Maybe. But this part of the country's a real attraction to three-wheelers, and the hills are full of prospectors."

Lyndsay frowned. "Prospectors? You mean for gold?"

"Uranium, mostly."

Lyndsay's attention quickened. "You know, a lot of places that the Indians used to call 'holy' were actually mildly radioactive—rich in uranium deposits. Maybe..."

But he was already nodding. "I know. That was my first thought, too. I even had the place assayed once, and turns out there is a little uranium in these rocks. Unfortunately, it'd cost more to get out than it's worth."

His expression was briefly shadowed as he added, "I even wondered if that wasn't what your father meant by 'untold wealth beneath this ground.' That was one of the things I wanted to ask him."

Lyndsay felt a stab of guilt and was for a moment tempted to tell him the truth—that her father had been dousing for water, not treasure. She resisted the temptation.

And then something struck her. She looked at him. "*You* had it assayed? You own this land?"

Jed's jaw tightened briefly as he realized his mistake, then, after a moment, relaxed. "I'm not the first treasure hunter in my family," he admitted reluctantly. "My mother says it's an inherited insanity. You can't blame my grandfather for getting excited—after all, he had the story, and the map, straight from the horse's mouth, as it were. But then my father narrowed the search area down and spent every last cent of his savings on this property. And me...well, I haven't held a job long enough to qualify for insurance benefits since I got out of the army. Sometimes I wonder if that map wasn't more of a curse than a gift to this family."

Lyndsay stifled a groan and practically writhed with guilt. Three generations of searchers, every last cent...

Get hold of yourself, she told herself sternly. After all, it wasn't *her* fault the Donovans were a family of dreamers. And it wasn't as though *she* had stolen their life savings...or even persuaded them to invest it in a barren stretch of rocky mesa. It wasn't as though she was stealing anything, really....

Except maybe a dream.

She mumbled uncomfortably, "Too bad about the uranium."

He cast her a questioning look at the apparent non sequitur.

"What I mean is, at least then your father's investment would've paid off."

"It still will," he assured her confidently. "The gold is out there. And I'm a lot closer to finding it than my father was, or my grandfather." He glanced at her with a smile that seemed deliberately provocative. "Aren't I?"

Lyndsay's returned smile was a little weak, and then faded altogether as they rounded a curve in the hilly terrain and she saw the place that, heretofore had been nothing but a couple of landmarks on an imaginary map in her head.

There was always a certain sense of excitement, even breathlessness, at the site of a new dig. But it was more than that.

They were at the bottom of a small canyon—small for these parts, anyway. Sheer rock walls rose to the east and west, a gentler slope toward the north. The perfect place for an ambush, Lyndsay thought.

There was just enough grass to indicate a water source nearby, but mostly the ground was covered with rocks and scrub brush. A travel trailer was nestled close to the western wall of the canyon, and nearby were a couple of pieces of earth-moving equipment. The ground bore the scars of previous failed and no doubt poorly thought-out excavations, a sight which would have normally provoked contemptuous disgust in Lyndsay. This time she barely noticed.

Jed brought the truck to a stop in front of the trailer, and her door was open before the vehicle completely stopped rolling. Jed said something to her, but she didn't hear. Lyndsay got out of the truck slowly, looking around.

It was the oddest thing. Generally she would have a feeling about a dig—good or bad, fruitless or fertile—that was for the most part based on research, experience and a practiced first impression of the terrain. Never before had she felt so *compelled* by a site.

But never before had two and a half million dollars been at stake.

The day was so still, the air so clear, she could hear the screech of a hawk as it circled overhead, so high it was barely a dash against the cerulean sky. The trailer, the modern equipment, even Jed seemed to fade away and she really *could* imagine it was 1870, and Joshua was coming down the pass.

She turned around, looking beyond the truck. He had probably come the way they had, for there couldn't be that many entrances into this canyon, even today. The cumbersome wagon he drove would've limited his choice of routes and made it imperative to have a hiding place ready.

Lyndsay walked along absently, retracing the route in her head. Joshua would have had no trouble spotting the landmarks once he entered the canyon. The streambed ran almost dead center down the middle of the canyon, though the width of its banks indicated it was much shallower today than it once had been. Automatically Lyndsay's eyes moved toward the northeastern shore, where the natural curvature of the land made a fork seem natural. Joshua would have followed the stream to its fork, from which point he would easily have been able to spot the dead tree, or perhaps he had sited the Widow-maker first, and used it as reference.

Lyndsay turned slowly on her heel, absently scanning the landscape, squinting a little in the sun. Then she stopped, staring. About midway up the northern slope, not as large as she had imagined it but clearly visible, was a dead tree.

It couldn't possibly be the same tree, of course. Jed would have mentioned it if it were—wouldn't he? But how could a dead tree remain standing against the forces of nature for a hundred years? It was impossible.

And just as she had decided the fantasy had gone far enough, Joshua Running Horse himself appeared against the skyline and started walking toward them.

Chapter Eight

He was a short, square man in faded denims and a rawhide vest. His dark hair was worn in two plaits beneath the rolled brim of his hat, and as he grew close enough for her to distinguish the broad strong features of his Native American ancestry she saw he was wearing a turquoise chunk pendant on a heavy silver chain.

Lyndsay stood mesmerized, trapped in time, as the man moved closer. Then he lifted his arm, grinning, and called, "Yo, Donovan!"

"Hey, *compadre!*" Jed shouted, so close behind her that Lyndsay jumped. *"¿Qué pasa?"*

The illusion was shattered, and Lyndsay gave an irritated shake of her head as Jed went forward to greet the newcomer.

The two men shook hands with the enthusiasm of two old friends.

"You're late this year."

"Ran into a few problems. How've you been?"

"Times are tough but I can't complain."

"And the wife?"

"Now *she* can complain. You never heard the like. But it's good to be back out here, isn't it?"

All during this interchange, the stranger's eyes never left Lyndsay, and his expression was one of polite curiosity as Jed led him forward with an arm slung around his shoulders.

"Gabe," Jed said, "this is Lyndsay Blake. Lyndsay, Gabe Blackwater. Gabe and his wife are camped on the other side of the canyon."

Gabe took off his hat, smiling. "It's a pleasure, miss. Jed recruited you for his treasure hunt, did he?"

"How do you do?" Lyndsay shook his hand.

Jed said, "Lyndsay's an archaeologist."

Gabe nodded, as though that explained everything. "Well, if you ever get a yen for civilized company, just come on downstream. My wife's name is Mary and she makes the best camp-stove biscuits this side of the Mississippi. Isn't that right, Jed?"

"No doubt about it. And you tell her I'll be over for some before the week's out."

Gabe grinned and replaced his hat. "It'll ease her mind to know you got here safe. I'll be getting on back, now. Just wanted to welcome you home."

He nodded in a pleasant way to Lyndsay. "Nice to meet you."

"Yes. Same here."

Lyndsay waited until he was out of earshot to say, "I thought you weren't interested in partners."

He turned back toward the truck. "I'm not."

"Then what's the deal with him?" She nodded toward Gabe's retreating figure. "He certainly seemed to know an awful lot about what's going on, and I thought you said this property was yours."

He lowered the tailgate and reached for a box of groceries. "Jealous?"

"Where my share of a million-dollar treasure is concerned—yeah, I guess I am."

Jed handed one of the boxes to her, grinning, and took another one for himself. "Don't worry, Gabe's not interested in the treasure."

Lyndsay gave a snort of disbelief. "Right."

Jed led the way toward the trailer. "And I don't own the whole canyon, just the part that's of interest to me. There's a good eight or ten acres that's still public land, and Gabe and his wife have been camping there for the past ten summers. They make good neighbors."

Jed took a key ring from his pocket and unlocked the trailer door. Though it stood in partial shade and the heat of the day had not yet reached its zenith, the blast of hot musty air that greeted them almost took Lyndsay's breath away.

The trailer was small and utilitarian, and efficiently arranged. Jed set down the groceries and turned on the air conditioner in the rear window, then opened the other three windows for ventilation. Lyndsay made a quick survey of the interior.

There was a cubbyhole of a kitchen with a narrow refrigerator and a small microwave and a hot plate. The bed was really more of a cot and the living area consisted of two chairs and a lamp table. A half-open door revealed a lavatory. There was a small closet with a sliding door, a built-in set of drawers and a small desk. All in all, the place was no bigger than the apartment she had left behind, and certainly no more comfortable.

Lyndsay wondered where he kept the map.

When her gaze returned to center again, she found him watching her, and there was no doubt in her mind that he knew exactly what she was thinking. He smiled.

"Sorry," he said, gesturing, "only one bed."

She smiled back. "I'm sorry, too" she said. "I brought my sleeping bag."

"I don't know..." He effected concern. "It can get kind of cool up here after the sun goes down."

He didn't move, but he seemed closer. Close enough to touch, really. Lyndsay was acutely aware of how small the room was.

She brushed past him to reach the bathroom, where she poked her head inside with a casual pretense of interest.

"No shower," she observed. "Where's a girl supposed to wash her hair?"

"Well," he said, "a girl can't have everything."

His voice was husky and close behind her. So close, in fact, that it made her skin prickle. When she turned from the bathroom, there wasn't a spare inch of space between him and the doorway. Her chest brushed his, an occurrence he did nothing to avoid. His hands settled on her waist.

"Particularly," he added, as his eyes drifted to her lips, "when she invites herself along for the ride without checking road conditions first."

Lyndsay's breath was shallow in her throat, her heartbeat quick. Perspiration pooled between her breasts, trickling down the midline. The air turned steamy.

Her hands moved with a will of their own to his waist, resting against the smooth leather of his belt. "Oh, but I'm along for a lot more than the ride."

A smile softened the corners of his lips, but she barely saw because his face was so close now, his features were a blur.

He murmured, "I'll just bet you are."

His breath skated across her mouth, so rich, so warm that she could not be sure the touch was not his lips, his tongue. She let her muscles weaken, just a little, and her eyes drift toward closing. She drew in a breath, imagining she could taste him. Her fingers caressed the soft cotton of his T-shirt, the firm muscles underneath. She felt heat and dampness, and the strong spare shape of male musculature.

She pushed away, fighting to bring her heartbeat, and her breathing, under control.

"We'd better bring in the rest of the stuff."

Her voice was not quite as strong as she would have liked. He acknowledged the fact with a smile.

After a moment, he let his hands drop, but not without a last lingering caress of her hips. "Right."

By the time they had unpacked the last box, they were both hot and sweaty and it was almost noon. Lyndsay had discovered the shower—an ecologically sound, solar-heated, outdoor contrivance—and was already having fantasies about it, when Jed reminded her pointedly that he had missed breakfast.

Lyndsay refused to take the hint. "Shall we draw straws for KP?"

"As my illustrious ancestor might have said, 'The only good thing about having a woman around the campfire is having somebody to cook for you.' And you're the woman."

"If that's all your illustrious ancestor thought women were good for," Lyndsay returned sweetly, "it's a wonder you were ever born. And you're the host."

"But you worked in a restaurant."

"That doesn't mean I can cook."

"You don't have to be a gourmet cook to put a sandwich together."

Lyndsay dug into her shorts' pocket for a coin. "Call it."

"Tails."

Lyndsay flipped the coin and caught it with a slap on the back of her hand. She showed it to him with a triumphant little smile.

He scowled. "All right. I'll make lunch. You do dinner."

"Wrong." She moved toward her duffel bag, which Jed had shoved into a corner. "You cook today, I'll cook tomorrow. We'll each make our own breakfast. Share the camp chores equally. It's the only way to avoid a breakdown of discipline."

"Sounds like a line from an army manual."

Lyndsay unzipped her duffel and took out a towel and a fresh bar of soap. "While you're making lunch," she said, "I'll take a quick shower. You weren't planning to do any digging today, were you?"

"No, I thought I'd sit around the pool and work on my tan. And thanks for offering to help put away the supplies."

She tossed a cocky grin at him. "Too many cooks..."

"I know, I know."

She *was* hot and sticky and a shower would feel nice, but that was not her main reason for choosing to shower in the middle of the day. When she returned, Jed would have to offer her privacy to dress, and it might be her last opportunity for a while to search the trailer in daylight. She might not discover where he kept the map, but she could go a long way toward finding out where it wasn't.

Jed was unpacking boxes as he spoke, and he turned with a bar of soap in his hand. He raised an eyebrow when he saw she was already provisioned. "You do come prepared, don't you?"

She smiled at him. "It's not my first time away from home."

Again she brushed against him as she moved past in the narrow space, and again he didn't try to do anything to avoid it. A low light, half teasing, half lustful, sparked his eyes as he said, "I may not be much of a cook, but I'm an expert back washer."

She lingered just long enough to give him her most provocative smile. "What a coincidence. So am I."

"I'll be happy to walk you to the shower."

"Thanks. I think I can find it," she assured him as she moved toward the door.

"Watch out for rattlesnakes."

She grinned over her shoulder. "You bet."

Grinning a little to himself, Jed turned back to the unpacking.

When he heard the creaky wooden door to the shower open, Jed figured he had about three minutes. Lyndsay was an experienced camper and wouldn't waste water, and she would hardly be spending much time powdering and primping out in the desert.

Jed dropped the box of cereal he was holding back in the box and hurried to Lyndsay's duffel bag. Quickly he opened it and, being careful not to noticeably disarrange anything, he went through the contents.

Cotton bikini panties—assorted colors. White cotton bras—front closure, he noted. Jeans, T-shirts, shorts. Shirts, a cardigan sweater, socks. Toiletries and a first-aid kit. And just as he was about to search again, certain he'd missed it, he felt a hard rectangular shape inside the folded sweater.

Carefully, trying not to make a jumble of her clothes, he removed a battered cordovan leather journal. With a lock.

He stared at it in equal mixtures of frustration and dismay. He should have known it wouldn't be that easy. Of course she wouldn't be carrying something as valuable as that diary around in her duffel bag unless it was locked.

On the other hand, those locks were notoriously flimsy.

Jed glanced quickly at the window nearest the shower, but saw no movement. He took the diary to the kitchen area, scrambling through the utility drawer for something—a knife, an ice pick, a meat skewer—small enough to use to pick the lock. He didn't want to break it unless he had to. He didn't know what he would find inside and he might still need her cooperation, which he would most certainly lose if she ever suspected he'd been spying.

He had his hand on the handle of a barbecue fork when he heard the door open behind him. Without glancing around he dropped the diary into the open drawer and put a box of crackers into the overhead cabinet.

"How about Vienna sausage and mustard?" he said.

"Sounds awful. How about five minutes to change my clothes?"

Jed turned, and there she was, wearing nothing but a skimpy white towel and a pair of desert boots. Her clothes were bundled over her arm and as he watched she kicked off the boots, moving barefoot across the linoleum to spread her clothes over the back of a chair.

"I hung my clothes on the wrong side of the shower stall and got them wet," she explained. "You really need to put up a hook or something."

The damp spots on the towel shadowed her figure provocatively, and when she bent slightly to arrange her shorts over the chair rail, Jed felt every muscle in his body strain to follow his gaze.

He was amazed at how normal his voice sounded. "They'll dry faster outside. There's a clothesline up."

"Is there? I didn't notice." She picked up her wet clothes and held them out to him, her expression innocent. "Would you mind?"

For one intense and deeply pleasurable moment Jed felt incapable of denying her anything. Then he remembered the diary. He couldn't leave her alone in here with that diary in the utility drawer. He had to get it back where it belonged before she discovered it was missing.

He turned casually back to the cabinet. "Why don't you change in the bathroom? I'll have lunch ready by the time you're finished." *And,* he added silently, *the diary back where it belongs.*

For a moment, Lyndsay was dumbfounded. She hadn't thought of the bathroom. But, then, she hadn't expected *him* to think of it, either—not while she was standing less than six feet away wrapped in nothing but a towel that barely covered the necessities.

She took her time rearranging her clothes on the chair, but she was thinking fast. She said, stalling for time, "No mustard, okay?"

Jed had his hand on the diary, planning to slip it back into place the minute she reached the bathroom. Out of the corner of his eye Jed saw her move toward the duffel bag instead and immediately realized the flaw in his plan: before she could get dressed, she would have to get her clothes. There was a chance she wouldn't notice the diary was missing, but not one he was willing to take. Not before he'd even had a chance to look at it.

In two steps and without thinking about it at all, he was beside her. From then on, it was pure instinct.

He touched her arm, brushing his fingers down its bare, still-damp length. "No promises," he said softly.

Lyndsay didn't know why she was surprised, but she was. She didn't know why the touch of his fingertips, trailing down her arm, should tingle like an electric shock, but it did.

She had no intention of offering him one iota of encouragement, or of allowing it to go a single step further, of course. But she lifted her eyes from his fingertips, still resting on her arm, to his face, and all her good intentions seemed to escape her.

She said huskily, "About what?"

"Mustard." His fingers drifted a little lower, entwining with hers in a brief, teasing gesture, then drifted even lower, across the terry cloth that covered her upper thigh, toying with the hem of the towel. "That was the subject, wasn't it?"

"Was it?" Her voice sounded breathless, and with good reason. His fingertips slipped beneath the towel, caressing her outer thigh, while his jeaned knee pushed gently between her legs, shifting his body even closer.

"Maybe not," he answered.

A moment ago the air-conditioning had been cool on her skin, but now his body heat covered her like a humid net. She couldn't look away from his face, and she felt an ache when she looked at him. He was good at this. So very good.

He lowered his head and she felt the brand of heat from his mouth, the press of her tongue. Weakness shot through her legs.

She lifted her arms to his neck for support. "I thought you were hungry," she managed.

"I am."

He closed his teeth on her bare shoulder, lightly at first, then with more pressure, and Lyndsay gasped with the sensation that spiraled through her and left her dizzy.

She thought, *Slow down. Wait. You should think about this*. . . .

And then his mouth covered hers and she didn't want to think about anything at all.

With his one arm Jed pulled her to him; the other hand still held the diary behind his back. It took more dexterity—and more power of concentration—than he had previously suspected he possessed to maneuver her to the floor. He guided their descent with one leg while supporting her with his arm and carefully, very carefully, reached out the hand that held the diary, searching for the duffel bag he knew was in the vicinity.

When her tongue darted inside his mouth, he thought his head would explode. He lost all concentration as, muffling a groan deep in his throat, he pressed her closer. Instinctively the hand that held the diary moved to caress her and he stopped himself just in time.

Blood was roaring in his head, his heart was thundering, breathing was something he had forgotten how to do. His hands—both of them—were like lead weights. When all he could think about was how her soft, supple flesh would feel against his palms, how her naked skin would press into his, how thin the towel was that separated them—when every nerve

GET A FREE TEDDY BEAR...

You'll love this plush, cuddly Teddy Bear, an adorable accessory for your dressing table, bookcase or desk. Measuring 5½" tall, he's soft and brown and has a bright red ribbon around his neck—he's completely captivating! And he's yours *absolutely free*, when you accept this no-risk offer!

AND FOUR FREE BOOKS!

Here's a chance to get **four free Harlequin American Romance® novels** from the Harlequin Reader Service®—so you can see for yourself that we're like **no ordinary book club!**

We'll send you four free books...but you never have to buy anything or remain a member any longer than you choose. You could even accept the free books and cancel immediately. In that case, you'll owe nothing and be under **no obligation!**

Find out for yourself why thousands of readers enjoy receiving books by mail from the Harlequin Reader Service. They like the **convenience of home delivery**...they like getting the best new novels months before they're available in bookstores...and they love our **discount prices!**

Try us and see! Return this card promptly. We'll send your free books and a free Teddy Bear, under the terms explained on the back. We hope you'll want to remain with the reader service—but the choice is always yours!

154 CIH AJAZ (U-H-AR-06/93)

► CLAIM YOUR FREE BOOKS AND FREE GIFT! RETURN THIS CARD TODAY! ►

NAME

ADDRESS   APT

CITY   STATE   ZIP

NO OBLIGATION TO BUY!

THE HARLEQUIN READER SERVICE: HERE'S HOW IT WORKS

Accepting free books puts you under no obligation to buy anything. You may keep the books and gift and return the shipping statement marked "cancel." If you do not cancel, about a month later we will send you 4 additional novels, and bill you just $2.71 each plus 25¢ delivery and applicable sales tax, if any*. That's the complete price—and compared to cover prices of $3.50 each—quite a bargain! You may cancel at any time, but if you choose to continue, every month we'll send you 4 more books, which you may either purchase at the discount price . . . or return at our expense and cancel your subscription.

* Terms and prices subject to change without notice.
  Sales tax applicable in N.Y.

and cell was drunk on her, he had little hope of persuading his body to take commands from his mind.

But somehow his searching, fumbling hand found the soft fabric of her duffel bag, found it open, felt the neatly folded clothing.... With her mouth open against his face, Lyndsay started to turn away, gasping for breath. Redoubling his passion, Jed covered her mouth with his again, lowering her backward, toward the floor.

He felt the folds of her sweater inside the duffel. Carefully, carefully, with a sound like a hurricane rushing in his ears, with his muscles straining, with the taste and feel and need for Lyndsay screaming through every nerve, he slipped the diary between its folds.

With equal care, he removed his hand. Relief swept through him and sensation heightened, flooded his awareness. He felt himself tumbling into the sensation of her, losing himself in her... And she stiffened in his arms.

Lyndsay tore her mouth away from his, gasping for breath, terrified by the intensity of the need she felt for him. She didn't even know this man, and what she did know about him was not to his advantage. She had come here to rob him, yet in another moment she would be lost in the throws of a mad animal passion, making love on the floor with a stranger who was quite possibly the most dangerous man she had ever known.

She placed her fingers across his lips, as much to protect herself from the need to seek them again as to silence whatever persuasive words he might utter. "No games, remember," she whispered, breathing hard. "Your rules."

Jed's first thought was that she had discovered him trying to return the diary, and a wave of self-loathing went through him that was so strong, desire all but withered in its wake. When he realized she had *not* found him out, he hated himself even more.

Damn, he thought, closing his eyes slowly. *Damn.* That was his rule—it had always been his rule—and he had broken it in a way more abominable than he had ever imagined possible. What kind of man was he anyway? Was the treasure that important to him?

I never meant it to go this far, Lyndsay, he thought. *I'm so sorry....*

He shifted his weight away from her, and Lyndsay sat up awkwardly, struggling to hold the scanty folds of the towel around her. In the process, her foot caught the duffel bag and knocked it over, spilling its carefully arranged contents on the floor. She didn't even notice.

She could hear Jed's harsh breath, as ragged and uneven as her own. How had this gotten so out of hand? Why did she feel as though she'd made the biggest mistake of her life . . . not for starting it, but for stopping it?

She said, "Jed, I—"

She never knew how she might have finished that sentence.

Jed said gruffly, ''I think I'll shower, too.''

Abruptly, without looking at her again, he left the trailer.

Chapter Nine

It seemed to be a long time after he had gone that Lyndsay still sat there, drawing in deep breaths, trying to stop the shivers that coursed along her nerve network like cobwebs being stirred by a breeze. *Close call,* she kept telling herself, but it felt like more than that. It felt as though she had just let the only thing she had ever wanted walk out the door, and she hated herself for that. Almost as much as she hated what she had to do next.

She moved on quickly to her duffel bag, whose contents had somehow ended up scattered on the floor. She pulled on shorts and a shirt and shoved the rest of the items haphazardly back into the bag. She glanced over her shoulder at the door. No sign of Jed.

She started with the most obvious places first. There were two kitchen drawers, each one of which squeaked slightly when opened and caused her to cringe. Neither of them contained anything but the expected tableware and kitchen supplies, and the undersides were clean.

She searched the cabinets next, muffling squeaky hinges with her hand. Fortunately he hadn't finished unpacking the supplies, so the search was easy.

She didn't really think he would chance keeping anything as fragile as an old map in the freezer, but she checked anyway. Nothing. Same for the toilet tank.

When she returned to the main room the shower water stopped running. There would be only a few safe minutes to search. But she had to take the chance and continue.

She couldn't drag this thing out anymore. Now, more than ever, she felt the urgency to get the map and get out of here. Now, before the temptation to stay became too strong, before she was dragged into his wild schemes and crazy dreams of forgotten treasure....

She knelt and carefully slid open the drawers beside the bed, moving quickly but quietly. They were empty. She swept her hand underneath and behind them. Nothing...

"It's not there."

At the sound of Jed's voice behind her, Lyndsay stood up, turning with a forced smile. "I was wondering if you had a fingernail file."

"What for?" He stood leaning against the door frame, his wet hair finger-smoothed over his scalp, his shirt open over a bare chest and clinging to his damp skin in patches. His expression was mild but his voice didn't hold much humor. "So you could stab me in the back literally as well as figuratively?"

Lyndsay stiffened and swallowed hard. She felt dull color creep into her cheeks.

He walked barefoot to the refrigerator and Lyndsay's eyes were riveted as he opened the door. She hadn't searched there.

But all he took out was a beer. He smiled at her. "Not there, either." He gestured with the can. "Want one?"

"Sure. Why not?"

He took out another beer and tossed it to her. She caught it easily and pulled the tab.

Jed leaned against the counter and sipped from the can, watching her. "Well," he said.

"Well." She held his gaze for a moment, then glanced down at the beer in her hand. She took a sip. Bravely she met his eyes. "You were right. I was looking for the map. But I don't think I ever misled you about what I wanted from you, did I, Donovan?"

Now Jed dropped his gaze. "No," he said quietly. "You didn't."

He looked back at her. "Listen," he said, with difficulty. "About what happened a few minutes ago..."

"Yeah, I know." Lyndsay's reply was swift and meant to dismiss the subject, but she knew it could not be done so easily. Something important had happened—or almost happened—between them and they couldn't ignore that.

Lyndsay glanced down at the beer can, absently gathering surface drops of moisture with her fingers. She could feel Jed's gaze on her, wary and watchful. She didn't know what to say, so she tried the truth.

"It's no secret I find you attractive," she said. She was only able to meet his eyes for an instant. "I guess it was partly my fault."

Jed felt a stab of remorse, mixed in with a good dose of guilt, that he couldn't dismiss. How far would he have let it go if Lyndsay hadn't had the good sense to stop him? Would he have regained his self-control at some point, or would he have let a not-so-admirable ruse get completely out of hand? He liked to think that he was more moral than that, but surely he had known the minute he'd taken her in his arms where it would end.

And for the same reason he couldn't pretend righteous indignation when he found her searching for the map, he could not ignore what she was feeling now. Or pretend he didn't understand it.

We're two of a kind, he thought. But he wasn't sure that was a good thing.

He took a sip of his beer. "You wanted to distract me, so you could look for the map. I guess you did that."

"And you wanted to distract me," she replied steadily, "so you could put the diary back in my bag. I guess you did that."

The shock in Jed's eyes was swift and genuine, and became only slowly mitigated by amazement. "Good God, woman," he said softly.

She managed a weak dismissing shrug. "I knew you hadn't had time to break the lock."

He gave a small shake of his head. "We're a couple of rotten characters, aren't we?"

Lyndsay smiled. "You know what they say. It takes a thief..." She let the rest trail off.

Jed looked down at the floor again, then back at her.

"Look," he said, a little gruffly. "I didn't mean for it to get out of hand. I wouldn't have...at least I don't think I would have." He made a vague gesture toward the floor. "Believe it or not, I usually have more finesse."

Lyndsay had not noticed a significant lack of finesse, but she thought it best not to tell him so.

She took a deep, somewhat unsteady, breath. She knew what she had to say next; she simply didn't know why it should be so difficult. Her choices were simple, really: the most perfect man who had ever crossed her path, or twenty thousand dollars.

She had come here for one reason, and the sooner she did what she had to do and got out of here, the better. She refused to get sidetracked now.

She pressed the beer can to her forehead briefly as though to cool herself; the small room in fact was quite well air-conditioned and what she was really trying to cool was her fevered thoughts. She muttered, without meaning to at all, "That was always my dad's problem. He kept getting sidetracked."

"What?"

Lyndsay looked at him, startled to have spoken out loud. She gave herself a mental shake and cleared her throat. "What I mean is, we probably need to make some rules."

The quiet watchfulness in Jed's eyes kindled a slow fire in the pit of her stomach. She couldn't prevent the path her own gaze took—over his bare chest and down the silky pattern of hair that narrowed and disappeared beneath the open buckle of his jeans. Her fingers remembered every curve of every muscle, every plane and angle, the softness and the hardness, the roughness and the satin. Her fingers remembered, and wanted to explore again.

"What kind of rules?" he asked cautiously.

She had to force her mind to focus. "It's probably best if we keep things strictly business between us. I mean, neither one of us is interested in a romance, no matter how tempting it might be. We do have to work together and that'll be a lot easier if we don't—well, complicate things unnecessarily."

Jed did not say anything for a long moment, and his face betrayed no reaction. Inside, he was in turmoil.

His instinctive reaction was violent protest, instant denial. That reaction was dictated by his body, whose needs were strong and whose sensate memory was not to be ignored. But equally strong were the dictates of logic, which told him this was the best thing that could have happened, the only way to deal with her until he got what he needed from her, and he should thank his lucky stars she had provided the solution instead of forcing him to do so.

Unfortunately, of course, he now needed two things from her. Logic aside, it was no longer quite so easy to determine which one was more important.

The only reason he had gotten entangled with her in the first place was because of the diary of course, and it was of primary importance that he get a look at it. He *had* to keep her around until he was able to do that.

But this afternoon he had discovered she could offer him more—much more—than just the key to enormous wealth. Was it greedy of him to want it all?

Jed knew the dangers of becoming involved with a woman like Lyndsay. The sexual attraction was only a fraction of the whole. The real danger lay within Lyndsay herself—her quick clever mind, her sharp tongue, her mysterious, even underhanded, nature. The excitement he felt just being around her, the possibilities she generated with her simple presence . . . those were the real snares.

A woman like Lyndsay could change his life, and Jed was not ready for that. That was the real trouble.

Of course, not that he was looking for a woman like Lyndsay. Not that he was looking for a woman at all.

So he said, quite casually, considering the turmoil that churned inside him, "You're probably right. I generally sleep outside in fair weather anyway, so you can have the bed." He finished off the beer and tossed the can into an empty box. "What's the point of camping if you have a roof over your head, right?"

Lyndsay was not at all sure she appreciated his easy acceptance of her decision. In fact, she was almost sure she resented it a great deal. Rarely had she felt so deflated, and it took all of her self-control to keep her voice light.

"Great. No problem, then. After all, we've got a job to do."

"Yep." He turned back toward the freezer. "I know it's early, but I'm going to throw a couple of these frozen dinners in the microwave. Then we'll sit down and talk about the dig. Not enough daylight left to do much else today."

"Sure."

Lyndsay drained her own beer, doing her best to adjust to his mood and finding it a great deal more difficult than she had thought. Why did men and women have to be so *different?* Didn't he have any emotions at all?

She nudged one of the boxes on the floor with her toe. "I'll help you square away some of this stuff. Any particular order?"

"Wherever you can find a place."

Jed pushed the button that started the microwave, then turned to her with a grin. "Hey," he said softly, "we'd be great together though, wouldn't we?"

Lyndsay felt her shoulders relax; her whole body relaxed with the tingling warmth of his grin, the memory in his eyes. Two steps closer and she would have melted into his arms.

"Out of this world," she agreed.

Their eyes lingered on one another's a moment longer, and the yearning that built between them was almost a palpable thing. Then Lyndsay turned away quickly, and started unpacking the boxes.

Chapter Ten

The attitude between them as they ate their microwave dinners was not exactly relaxed, but it was a little more comfortable than Lyndsay had expected under the circumstances. Jed produced a folding card table from under the bed and they ate sitting across from one another with a large multicolored topographical sketch of the canyon between them. As they ate, Jed used the tip of a pencil to point out the areas he had previously explored.

"These lines here," he said, indicating a series of yellow symbols, "are where I've superimposed the results of the geographic survey." He took a bit of turkey and dressing and chewed. "The usual. Shale, limestone. The whole canyon is riddled with caves and canyons."

Lyndsay stared at him, amazed that he could say it so casually. "Well, that's it, then, don't you think? Joshua had to have hidden the treasure in a cave. He didn't have time to bury it. If you've got the geographical survey—"

Jed just smiled. "All we have to do is figure out which one of the several thousand caves or corridors he picked, then figure out how to get into it. Most of them are deep underground, or sealed off by ancient landslides fifteen, twenty feet thick."

Now Lyndsay's amazement was from a different source, and mingled with dismay. "You really have spared no expense, have you? I'm just a little surprised you didn't commission satellite photos."

Jed's expression remained diffident. "I didn't commission them, but I did manage to get copies of the relevant pictures—infrared, depth sensitive. They didn't tell me much I didn't already know."

There was a sinking feeling in Lyndsay's stomach. "Geographic surveys, satellite photos... You really *have* tried everything."

He shrugged. "The way I see it, it's like what they say about medicine—if you live long enough, they'll eventually find a cure for whatever's killing you. Three generations of my family have been looking for this treasure. I figure if we look long enough, technology will eventually catch up with us and show us right where Joshua left it.

"Meantime..." He finished the last of his dinner, scraping the tin plate. "There's no substitute for a good old-fashioned pick and shovel." And he cocked an eyebrow at her. "Now do you see why I said I didn't need an archaeologist to tell me how to dig?"

Lyndsay nodded and pretended to concentrate on her meal, but it was not her own usefulness—or lack of the same—on this trip that was bothering her. It was Jed.

Dedication, enthusiasm, commitment... Those were not qualities that commonly would be thought of as undesirable in a man. But seeing them in Jed, and knowing their source, filled Lyndsay with despair.

She had always suspected this might be more than a hobby for him. But she had not realized how closely his conviction bordered on obsession. He really believed the treasure was out there. More than that, he was convinced that he, and only he, could find it.

Lyndsay had lived most of her life with a man with a mission. A man of vision, conviction, passion for his own lost causes. A man who had sacrificed greatness for obsession. A man who was completely wrong.

She couldn't go through that again.

Not, of course, that it made any difference to her what Jed Donovan's personal passions were, nor how wrong he might be. Her interests began and ended with the map, and if he wanted to go off the deep end with satellite photos and ground surveys, that was his business. He was a means to an end; that was all.

It was a great deal easier to persuade herself of that now, sitting across a table from him, than it had been an hour ago in his arms. But the fact was, she still was not entirely successful.

She picked up their empty trays and beer cans and carried them to the trash, more to give herself a chance to move away from his disturbing proximity than out of any sense of domestic habit.

"What are you going to do with the treasure when you find it?" she asked.

He grinned. "Well, I *won't* be sharing it with Uncle Sam, I'll tell you that."

Lyndsay gave a grimace of agreement. Tax laws regarding treasure and salvage were notoriously punitive, which was why so many such operations were conducted illegally.

"One good reason for not taking on a partner," she pointed out.

"Right. It's not easy to find someone with just the right amount of ethics on top of a cunning criminal mind."

"I'm flattered to qualify."

The expression in his eyes was speculative, though the smile remained. It made Lyndsay just the smallest bit uneasy, even as a tingle of cautious excitement began low in her stomach.

"I didn't say you did," he said. "Yet."

Lyndsay lifted an eyebrow. "Which part is in doubt? The criminal mind or the ethics?"

"Loyalty," he answered without hesitation, his gaze unwavering.

Lyndsay was not at all sure how to take that, or how he meant her to take it. She decided to discontinue the subject for the moment.

She opened a cabinet. "What's for dessert?"

"Damn," he answered mildly. "I meant to whip up a flan, but time just got away from me."

She opened a bag of licorice whips and took out a couple. "Want one?"

"Not my style. I'll take another beer, as long as you're up."

Lyndsay hesitated, then opened the refrigerator door. The sooner he drank up all the beer, the sooner he'd go back into town and give her a chance for a genuine search. Besides that it had been a long time since she'd had a chance to wait on a man—outside the course of her duties at the café, of course. She found she missed it.

"Don't let this become a habit," she told him, setting the can before him. "It's not in my job description."

She resumed her seat across from him, chewing absently on the licorice whip as she returned her attention to the canyon drawing. "I wouldn't turn you in to the IRS, by the way," she said. "It'd only cause trouble for me."

"An interesting definition of loyalty," he mused. "Only stab your partner in the back if it doesn't cause any trouble for yourself. I think I like it."

"Are these little red *X*'s where you've already dug?"

"That's right."

The shorts Lyndsay wore beneath the baggy shirt were knee length and loose fitting, and her hair was tied back at the nape of her neck with an elastic band. Frowning over the sketch, chewing on licorice, there should have been nothing sexual about her at all.

But everything about her exuded sexuality and, for Jed, always would. Her head, bent over the paper, was close enough for him to smell her shampoo and the scent brought back a flood tide of sensual images. Her lips, pursed around the candy, the open collar of her shirt and the hint of collarbone it revealed, the simple knowledge that she probably was not wearing a bra beneath. When just sitting beside her was torture, how did he expect to be able to stay here alone with her in the desert for untold days—and nights?

Men thought women were the foolish ones, the sentimental ones, the romantics. But all Jed had to do was smell her hair and his knees went weak. And, instead of trying to figure out how to get some time alone with that diary so he could find out what he needed to know and be rid of her, Jed's mind had been repeatedly turning, over the past hour, to the question of how to get her to stay. It was crazy.

But half of two and a half million dollars was still a hell of a lot of money.

And that was when he really became alarmed. He had never considered sharing the find before, not with anyone. All he'd ever wanted from her was what was inside that diary. Could he really allow the events of one afternoon to jumble his thinking that badly?

"What would you do with it?" he said.

She glanced up at him questioningly.

"The money."

The shadow that crossed her face, the way she quickly evaded his eyes, was far too easy to read, and he smiled.

"You don't believe there is a treasure, do you?"

She said, a little too quickly, "Of course I believe it."

Then, seeing the tolerant and far-too-perceptive look in his eyes, she capitulated. It was getting harder to hide anything from him, and that was extremely unnerving.

She could only hope this unfortunate tendency toward honesty didn't get any worse, even as she admitted, "I'm a little cynical, okay? It comes from too many years of watching my father throw away his life chasing down dreams. Yes, there's probably a treasure. And yes, your chances of finding it are a little bit better than the average Joe's. But still, you said yourself, three generations have tried and turned up nothing. God knows you've tried everything in the book and you're still no closer...."

"Of course I am. I've got you now. And you've got the diary."

Mercifully, Lyndsay didn't flinch. Perhaps it was the surprise of hearing "I've got you now"—so possessive, so sure, so wonderfully personal—that sent her mind tumbling down unfamiliar paths and caused her perception to be just a beat or two behind in picking up on the next part of his statement.

And by the time she understood what he meant, she was too well controlled to let her disappointment show. He didn't have her. He didn't *want* her, not in that sense. What he wanted—what he had—was the diary.

Or so he thought.

She said, "I told you before, there might not be anything there that can help you at all."

His gaze was steady. "There's only one way to find out, isn't there?"

Lyndsay managed a smile. "You might not guess from my behavior this afternoon, but I *do* know when to hold on to my assets."

He looked at her soberly for a long moment. Then he got up and crossed the room.

Lyndsay watched, chewing on the licorice to soothe the attack of nerves that had been brought on by the close call, as he stood on the bed.

"What are you doing?"

"One of us has got to trust the other sooner or later."

Nerves gave way to curiosity as he reached overhead and dislodged one of the ceiling tiles, then to heart-pounding excitement as he brought a package out of the recess.

The map.

Jed stepped down from the bed, his expression absurdly relaxed for such a momentous occasion. "Guess it'd better be sooner."

The licorice felt sticky in her mouth and Lyndsay swallowed hard as he came over to her, bearing a clear plastic bag with what appeared to be a red towel inside. She was surprised at the slight hoarseness of her tone that even being near so precious an artifact could cause.

"That's the stupidest hiding place I've ever seen," she said.

"You didn't find it."

She scowled. "I would have if I'd had time. Besides, what if there was a fire, or a tornado, and you *know* how prone to flooding these canyons are." Her indignation was rising, as it always did in defense of the ancient, the irreplaceable, the milestones of history. "You never should have hidden it inside! Anything could've happened."

Jed was unconcerned as he sat down at the table and opened the bag. "Doesn't matter. I've got it all up here, anyway." He tapped his head. "This is a family heirloom, that's all."

Lyndsay would have had a great deal more to say on the subject of his cavalier attitude about something that was worth twenty thousand dollars, but he began unwrapping the package, and anticipation left her speechless.

There were several more layers of plastic wrap around the towel, and Lyndsay had to grudgingly give him credit for that. Inside the red towel was a layer of white flannel, and when that was peeled away... the map.

It looked amazingly familiar to Lyndsay, exactly how she had imagined it. Still, there was a slight tremor to her hand as she reached out to touch it. Jed had no such reverence for the stuff of which the past was made, and he handed it over casually.

It was a square of animal hide, exceptionally well tanned and softened over the years to a texture that was almost velvet. The color had once been a pale cordovan, but the oil from many hands had settled in over the years to splotch the fabric dark brown. The map itself was burned into the leather, not drawn on, which was fortunate, because any such drawing would have long since been rubbed away.

"This is very old," she said hoarsely.

Lyndsay was hardly even aware of having spoken. Her gaze was frozen on the piece of leather in her hands, but what she was really seeing was something else entirely... a smooth brown hand, etching the symbols into the hide with a smoking stylus. Golden brown torso, straight dark hair and in the background, stately buildings of timber and stone. A village, but not an Indian village. Egypt?

"Over a hundred years," Jed agreed easily.

Not Egypt, she thought, *even older. . . .*

And then her eyes focused on the map again, and on Jed's words, and she was annoyed with herself. It was old, yes, but not ancient. And it must have been those strange markings on the side that had reminded her of Egyptian hieroglyphics, and set her mind to wandering.

Her experienced eye could date the map at just about what Jed claimed. Old, but not ancient. Why was there a part of her that persisted in thinking that this was only a copy of a map that was much, much older?

Which was ridiculous of course.

"Do you read Creek?" she asked.

"Just enough to read that map."

"And you're sure these are Creek symbols?"

"Yep."

"What does it say?"

Jed dragged his chair close to hers to better see the direction her finger was pointing. His nearness was a distraction even for the excitement of finding the map, of having it in her hands.

He had pulled on a T-shirt, but it was the same one he had so hastily discarded earlier, and each wrinkle told its own story. His hair, too, was still rumpled from the afternoon, and his scent . . . His scent was in her pores, on her tongue, in her hair, every part of her.

Why are we doing this? she thought helplessly. *Why are we wasting time with old maps and lost treasures when we could be doing what men and women were meant to do—discovering each other, pleasuring each other, loving each other.*

"All of this," Jed said, indicating a row of characters, "is the ID, like the bar code at a supermarket. The name of the tribe, clan, family and so forth who's in charge of the map. Then it waxes poetic, "Keeper of the mysteries passed down from the Old Ones, charged to deliver unto the People their rightful heritage."

Lyndsay felt a shiver go down her spine. She stared at Jed. "You said—Old Ones?"

He gave her an odd look. "That's right. Why?"

"Nothing. It's just...something about this map made me think it might be even older than it is, and now, that writing seems to suggest that a 'mystery was passed down'...like this might be a copy of an even older map."

He frowned. "That doesn't make any sense."

Lyndsay knew that, and it frustrated her. "Donovan, did you ever really think Joshua made this map?"

He looked a little uncomfortable. "He could have."

"Why in the world," Lyndsay demanded, exasperated, "would a man in 1870 take the time and trouble to burn a map into a piece of tanned hide if all he was going to do was use it to remind himself where he'd hidden something? Much less put all that folderol about tribe and heritage and mystery on it."

The line between Jed's brows deepened slightly even as he tried to shrug it off. "Hell, I don't know. Indians love that ceremonial crap. Maybe he just did it for decoration."

Lyndsay gave him a long and withering look.

Jed said impatiently, "All right, so I have no imagination. I don't really care who drew the map or why. The important thing is who has it now."

"That," Lyndsay told him acerbically, "is what you need an archaeologist for. 'Who' and 'why' are always important. Sometimes they make all the difference in the world as to how data is interpreted—or whether it's uncovered at all."

She looked at the map thoughtfully. "Joshua was coming from Oklahoma. It's likely he might have heard of this 'holy ground' but there's no reason he'd have to know exactly where it was. This might be a part of a larger map, something the tribe kept with them, like a collection of holy places."

"There was never anything like that," Jed said dismissively. "Besides the Creek were never in Colorado."

Lyndsay decided to ignore that for the moment. "See, the map points out all the entrances to the canyon. Funny how little the topography has changed in all these years, isn't it?"

"It's changed too much to suit me," Jed muttered.

Lyndsay studied the map in silence for a while. It was really very simple, as maps went. The stream was easy to interpret, its fork plainly visible. Directly across from it was a jumble of spirals and loops that weren't quite so easy to interpret, but which Lyndsay took to be indicative of the canyon wall. In the midst of these loops, approximately thirty degrees to the south of the fork in the stream, was another hieroglyph which must have represented the magic rock. What had Jed called it? Whispering Rock.

On the opposite side of the canyon, in amazing proximity to the place where Lyndsay had noticed that other dead tree this afternoon, was the Widowmaker. From each of the three major landmarks a line was drawn, forming a rough triangle. The third point of the triangle was the rock, and from that a line was drawn to the opposite wall of the canyon, terminating in a crude sunburst design.

"*X* marks the spot," Lyndsay murmured. "Or in this case, a sunburst."

It would be apparent even to an amateur—which Lyndsay most certainly was not—that the only important landmark on the map was the rock. The stream and the tree were only included to provide reference points for the third point in the triangle. Once that was located, the map line drawn to the opposite wall was like a surveyor's reference mark, pointing directly to the treasure.

Lyndsay stood up slowly, still studying the map. "It can't be that easy," she muttered.

"What?"

Jed rose, too, and followed her to the door.

Lyndsay refused to allow herself to get too excited; the whole thing was just too obvious.

"You must have checked it out," she said. "I mean, you can see where the streambed forks, and if that dead tree is in the same place in relationship to it as the one on the map..."

"What tree?" Jed said, frowning.

Lyndsay stepped outside, consulting the map once again to get her bearings, and moved away from the trailer. She turned toward the dead tree she had seen that morning, and lifted her arm to point it out.

It was no longer there.

"In the first place," Jed said "the stream doesn't fork anymore. If it did, that would give me at least one landmark to go on. But erosion has worn down the streambed to the point that it's hard to even guess where the fork might once have been. As for the Widowmaker...if that's what you're talking about—"

"It was here this morning," Lyndsay said.

Jed stared at her.

Lyndsay felt herself grow chilled as she gazed into the empty distance, focusing her eyes as though sheer effort could make the tree reappear. It *had* been there that morning, she was certain of it. It *had*.

Lyndsay turned full circle, on the off chance that she might have mistaken her bearings. Though it was after six, there was plenty of daylight left and she could clearly see that everything was exactly as she remembered. But the dead tree that had so caught her attention that afternoon was no longer there.

And neither was the fork in the stream.

"Weird," Lyndsay mumbled. "This is really weird."

That was of course a deliberate understatement. Her heart was pounding, her palms felt sweaty and she simply couldn't believe her eyes. Trees didn't just disappear. Neither did streams. *Nothing* was as she remembered it. Could she have imagined everything this morning?

With the map in her hand, she walked down to the stream. It was only about twenty feet from the trailer, shallow and meandering. It made a pleasant sound as it splashed against the flat rocks in its path, but as far as she could see there was no fork.

"Let me get this straight," Jed said behind her. "When you got here this morning you walked down and saw—"

"Of course I didn't walk down," she snapped. "I was just looking out over the land from the truck."

"And you saw the fork in the stream?"

She must have imagined it. She must have somehow superimposed what she knew about the map onto the existing landscape and *imagined* the terrain as it had been a hundred years ago. The mind was a powerful thing and not always predictable. But she didn't like it. Not one bit.

She scowled. "Obviously I didn't. See how it's wider in some places than in others? It must have been an optical illusion. And over there, at the slope of the canyon, I saw a dead tree, so naturally I tried to make the two line up.''

''And did they?''

She shrugged, more disturbed than she wanted to admit. ''I thought they did, pretty much the same way they do on this map.''

Jed scanned the canyon wall. ''So where's the tree?''

''Maybe it fell down,'' she retorted. ''It was dead, after all.''

Jed just looked at her, so she raised an impatient arm in the direction of the now-absent tree. ''It was over there,'' she said. ''Between those two rocks that look like old men's faces. Dead center. And the stream looked like it forked right over there, where that clump of weeds starts.''

Jed had taken the map from her, and was studying it as she spoke. His expression was thoughtful as he gazed from the stream to the slope of the canyon, then back to the map. Then he shrugged, casually folding the map.

''It doesn't make any difference anyway,'' he said. ''It couldn't have been the same tree.''

''That's what I thought,'' Lyndsay said, but that was faint comfort.

And as she watched Jed fold the map again and tuck it into his shirt pocket, she was gripped with another kind of dismay. She had been that close, and she let it get away. She had held the map in her hand, she had let herself be distracted by optical illusions and imaginary trees, and she might never get a chance like that again.

She was beginning to wonder if she was really cut out for this kind of work.

On the other hand, she decided, cheering fractionally, she couldn't exactly hit Jed over the head and make off with the map in broad daylight. She would just have to keep her eye on the map—and on Jed—and pick her time. It would come soon enough.

Jed touched her shoulder, gesturing that they should return to the trailer. It was an ordinary gesture, commonplace enough to be considered impersonal, but Lyndsay's reaction could not have been more intense had his fingertips been charged with electricity. There was a moment of hesitation, of full awareness, of decision. And then his hand slid down to her waist.

Lyndsay put one foot in front of the other very casually, she walked beside him with every appearance of ease. But every sense she possessed was riveted to his nearness, his scent, his body heat, his touch. The brush of his jeaned hip against hers, the flexing of strong fingers as they curved into the slight indentation of her waist. There was a comfortable possessiveness to his touch that made her breath quicken, and it took all her willpower to fight the urge to slip her arm around his waist, and lay her head back against his shoulder.

A moment later she was glad she had resisted the impulse.

"I showed you mine," Jed said. "Don't you think it's time you showed me yours?"

Lyndsay gave a startled laugh, glancing up at him. "What?"

"The diary," Jed explained mildly. "If it has anything at all to say, now's the time for me to hear it."

Lyndsay tried to disguise her discomfort, but the stiffening of her muscles was instinctive. Jed was so attuned to her that he felt it immediately; she was so attuned to him, she felt his reaction at the same time. Once again they were guarded and watchful, fencing around each other, more like wary—if respectful—enemies than lovers, or even partners.

Lyndsay hated that.

"I told you," she said shortly. "A man's diary is personal, and I don't want anyone reading it but me."

Jed dropped his hand from her waist, his exasperation clear. "For God's sake, what could possibly be in there that would embarrass him now? Or you, for that matter?"

Lyndsay faced him squarely, and it was the hardest thing she had ever had to do. God, how had she ever gotten into this? How had she let it go so far, and how much longer could she keep it up?

She kept her tone cool despite the heat in her eyes. "That's precisely what is *not* your business."

There was genuine anger in his eyes now. "Look, we had a deal."

I'm sorry, Jed, she thought helplessly. *I wish I'd never started this. I wish . . . a lot of things.*

But she had started it, and she had no choice now but to see it through. It was for the best, she assured herself. It really was.

"The deal was," she reminded him curtly, "that I'd help you, and I will. But I'll do it *my* way."

"Since when?" he demanded.

She managed a tight smile. "Since always."

But Jed was not amused. "And I thought *I* was a son of a bitch," he said quietly. His eyes were probing. "What the hell kind of woman are you anyway?"

The words, the distant, calculating look in his eyes stabbed at her, hitting her like a lead weight right in the breastbone. Was there anything more painful than seeing that look in the eyes of a man with whom you were rapidly falling in love? Especially when it was deserved.

Damn it, she thought, fighting back the stinging mist that wanted to rise out of her chest and into her eyes. She had known better. This was exactly what happened when she mixed business with pleasure, and she was getting what she deserved.

She swallowed, lifted her chin a fraction, and replied simply, "A smart one."

She brushed passed him toward the trailer.

Chapter Eleven

Lyndsay was in an open-air palace of some kind with ornately carved timber columns leafed in gold and silver. The room in which she stood was circular, and the view spread out before her on four sides was of a lush fertile valley surrounded by rugged mountains. The floor beneath her bare feet was cool polished marble, and she was nude except for a shimmery, transparent floor-length garment that tied at one shoulder.

In the distance she could hear the workmen returning from their day's work on the tunnel, and as she looked out over the beautiful valley she was filled with an almost overwhelming sense of sorrow and loss.

Lyndsay's conscious self wondered about this, because it was all so breathtakingly beautiful, almost utopian. Why should the sight of it make her sad?

She moved into another room, where a man was working at a long table littered with scraps of metals and precious stones. Her heart swelled with tenderness when she saw him. His bronzed shoulders were strong and powerful, his torso lean and perfectly sculpted. His thick brown hair fell below his shoulders and was held back with a silver circlet. He wore sandals on his feet and around his waist a breechclout fashioned out of woven metal forged so fine, its consistency was like cloth.

She came up behind him and dropped her hands to his shoulders. She said softly, "You continue to work when you know all this must be left behind."

He turned and smiled at her. "I've just finished a gift for you. I was going to save it for our wedding day, but you look so sad, I think I'll show it to you now."

He opened his hand and inside was a pair of linked bracelets worked in braided silver and gold, studded with tiny, perfectly cut chips of topaz. The craftsmanship was so delicate, the piece might have been made of sunshine and air, and just looking at it made her gasp with wonder.

She took it into her hands. "But—it doesn't open," she said, examining it. The bracelets seem to have been made one inside the other, separate but inseparable. "It won't fit over my hand, and there's no clasp. How do I get it on?"

He retrieved the piece, green eyes twinkling. "It opens," he assured her, "but only for the man who holds the key to your heart. And I will open it for you on our wedding day.''

LYNDSAY AWOKE, feeling sweaty and headachy, to the sound of the rhythmic clanging of machinery, with remnants of the disturbing but fast-disappearing dream still clinging to her like cobwebs.

She sat up in bed, pushing back her damp hair. The cause of her first discomfort was readily apparent, as she remembered she had turned off the air conditioner the night before and the morning sun, streaming through the window over the bed, had already warmed the room considerably.

The headache was just as quickly explained by squinting at her watch. It was only a little after seven o'clock and Lyndsay never, if she could possibly help it, rose before eight-thirty. And that noise.

She sat on her knees and looked out the window, rubbing her eyes against the morning light. When she could focus, she saw Jed, working on one of the pieces of earth-moving equipment. His shirt was off, and he was lying on his back in the dirt, trying to loosen a bolt on the underside of the bulldozer by tapping it with a wrench handle. As Lyndsay watched, he missed and struck his knuckles instead, which elicited a loud and colorful curse.

Lyndsay smiled as she turned from the window and went to make coffee.

She showered and dressed while the coffee was brewing, and when it was done she took her cup down to where Jed was working. By that time he had finished torturing the bolt and was working on the engine. Lyndsay stopped a few feet away and just watched him for a moment.

In the soft morning sun his torso was already glistening with sweat, his back streaked with dirt, his hair damp. The stubble on his face was thick enough to show golden glints, and there was oil on his hands. His jeans were unbelted and rode low on his hips, just below his navel, and with her eyes Lyndsay followed the narrow line of body hair as it disappeared beneath the material.

She was aware of a swelling pressure in her chest, the taste of longing, and she thought, for not the first time in the past twenty-four hours, *Not fair.*

She knew Jed was aware of her presence, but she was glad that he finished his work before looking at her. It gave her a chance to take a sip of her coffee and compose herself.

"What are you doing?" she asked.

He took a stained rag from his back pocket and wiped first his tools, then his hands. He nodded toward the bulldozer.

"Just getting the equipment ready to go."

She gestured around them. "How can you afford all this stuff, anyway?"

"Most of the equipment's rented for the season. Which is not to say this is a cheap hobby. Fortunately, mechanics—even part-time ones—are paid top dollar.''

''And every penny you make goes into this.''

''Right.''

Their conversation was impersonal and relaxed, but there was a gulf of unresolved emotion between them that had begun yesterday with unconsummated longing and had ended with unspoken accusations. And though both of them tried to ignore it, neither of them really could. Caution was evident in his eyes, and sorrow ached in her chest.

Lyndsay sighed and gave up the effort to pretend nothing was wrong. She said, ''They always say things will look better in the morning, but they never do, do they?''

''Sometimes they do. Sometimes they just look different.''

So close, Lyndsay thought. Yesterday she had been so close to closing her hands around something more precious than gold, and she had let it all slip away because she was too afraid to reach for it. She had lied to him, used him, taken his trust and refused to give back her own...yet still she hoped that he didn't hate her. That he might give her another chance.

Lyndsay's throat tightened even as her fingers tightened around the coffee cup. ''And how do they look to you this morning?''

He met her eyes easily, but his expression was unreadable. ''Different.''

She didn't know what that meant. She didn't know what to feel. He was wary of her as he had every right to be, and she had no right to ask for anything more.

Lyndsay took a breath. "This," she said flatly, "is why it's always a mistake to get personally involved with a business partner."

"I'll remember that in the future."

She could almost feel the effort it took for him to lighten his tone, to move on as though nothing of any importance had ever happened between them.

"In the meantime, though," he said, "I had an idea. And since it was partly your idea, I guess I have to let you in on it."

Lyndsay was puzzled. "My idea?"

For the first time, Jed smiled. Relief went through Lyndsay like butter melting in the sun.

"Yeah, I was a little surprised myself. That you actually contributed something useful to this project, that is."

On easier ground now, Lyndsay took a sip of the coffee. "I'm sure I didn't do it on purpose. What did I contribute?"

Jed focused his attention on cleaning the oil from under his fingernails with the rag. "I was up early this morning and, just for something to do, I took some compass readings on the places where you thought you saw that tree and stream fork, and used them to project a hypothetical position for Whispering Rock. Then, using the same angles and perspective, I made my own triangle and drew my own bisecting line, just like in the real map, just to see what would happen. Let me show you what I found.''

He tossed the dirt rag aside and pulled on his T-shirt. Casually he led the way across the canyon. They were almost out of sight of the trailer when he stopped.

''This is it?''

Lyndsay looked around at the piece of ground which, except for the expensive-looking metal detector leaning against a rock formation, was basically indistinguishable from any other part of the canyon.

''This is it.''

He picked up the metal detector and switched it on.

Lyndsay would have to have been a fool not to realize that he had brought her here for a purpose, even if the tension on Jed's face had not alerted her. Excitement wound like a wire through her nerves even though the only sound from the metal was the faint hum of its ordinary scanning.

Jed swept the device over the rock formation, over the ground where Lyndsay stood, in a three-foot arc to his left. But when he moved to the right, the metal detector began to beep, faintly at first, then more loudly until, when Jed held it at an angle close to the canyon wall, it began to screech.

Even though she was prepared for it, Lyndsay could not believe what she was seeing—and hearing. Her heart lurched, and coffee sloshed over her hand but she barely felt it. Her knees went weak. There was something there. There was *actually something there.*

Jed switched off the detector. Silence resounded. The morning seemed suddenly to sparkle with possibilities, with promise, with magic. *There was something there.*

It was a long time before Lyndsay could speak. When she could, it was only to joke feebly, "So what do you think? Somebody lost a watch?"

Jed had of course had more time to regulate his emotions and put the facts in perspective, and his expression was carefully schooled and noncommittal. But he couldn't hide the fire in his eyes; he could only keep it well banked.

"It's bigger than a watch," he said.

Lyndsay was a little breathless. "How big?"

"Big."

She could have strangled him for the obscurity, but this was no time to get into a fight over semantics. She was having enough difficulty just keeping her voice steady.

"Can you tell how deep it is?"

He looked back toward the spot on the canyon wall. "About fifteen feet. There's got to be some kind of cave or hole in the wall back there that's been covered over by shifting rock. The only way I can see to get to it is to dig."

Lyndsay released a low breath. "Wow. I didn't think those metal detectors could pick up anything that was buried deeper than a handful of change after a day at the beach."

"State-of-the-art," he replied briefly, still studying the hillside. "Of course, readings get distorted with that kind of depth. You can't tell a whole lot about what's in there, or even exactly what it is. The only thing to do is start scooping out the hillside."

"Excuse me?" Lyndsay stared at him. The excitement that fluttered within her spiraled to a stop. "You can't mean *that* was why you were tuning up your bulldozer?"

Irritation flashed in his eyes. "Why the hell else?"

"Are you crazy? You can't tackle a thing like this with a bulldozer! You could send the whole canyon into a landslide, not to mention—"

"Give me a break! I've been operating heavy equipment since—"

"Not to *mention*," she repeated heatedly, "the evidence that will be lost—"

"Evidence! This is a treasure hunt, not a crime scene."

"Listen to me—"

"No," he interrupted firmly, and with enough vehemence to startle Lyndsay into silence. "You listen to *me*. I'm in charge here. I know what I'm doing. I've been doing it for over fifteen years without any help from you."

"Well, it would seem to me you haven't quite got the hang of it yet. I don't see any treasure, do you?"

His jaw knotted briefly. "Don't push it, lady."

Lyndsay took a deep breath, and another. Forcefully she made her fingers relax around the coffee cup.

He had every right to be defensive, of course, after the way she had acted about the diary. He had no reason to trust her or even confide in her, much less share the treasure with her. Worst of all, he was probably right.

But more importantly, the sudden flare of tempers, the harsh words, had very little to do with the treasure or whose method was best for finding it. It had to do with wanting and denial, with hurt and betrayal, with their own separate struggles with better judgment.

Besides, who said there even *was* a treasure? The metal detector could be picking up anything from old mining equipment to a camper's steel tent pole. All she was interested in was the map. She had to keep reminding herself of that. If Jed wanted to bulldoze his way through the Grand Canyon, let him. It was none of her business.

"You're right," she said, with a fair imitation of contrition for one who used the expression so rarely. "This isn't an archaeological dig. You're the expert treasure hunter. Do it your way."

His expression grew suspicious. "I intend to."

She turned back toward the trailer. "I made a pot of coffee, if you want any. I'm going to get some breakfast."

She'd gone about half a dozen steps when his voice stopped her.

"Hey."

She glanced back.

He stood where she had left him, fingers tucked into his pockets, looking after her with a very peculiar expression on his face. "That's it? That's all you've got to say?"

She didn't precisely know what he was talking about. She shrugged.

"What difference does it make what I say? You won't listen anyway."

The curious, almost puzzled look in his eyes deepened fractionally, and he looked as though he wanted to say more. He even drew a breath to do so, but apparently changed his mind.

He answered only, "I'm going to put some of this equipment away. I'll be up in a minute."

WOMEN, JED THOUGHT three hours later. He'd never understand them. And maybe he should be glad that he didn't.

He'd been carefully working at the hillside with various pieces of earth-moving equipment for over an hour now. Progress was slow because a certain amount of planning, calculation and care *was* required to avoid a landslide that, at best, could be self-defeating and at worse extremely dangerous.

For the same amount of time, Lyndsay had been patiently taking the rubble, bucketful by bucketful, from the pile he had created, moving it to her own, smaller pile some ten feet away. He watched her fill her bucket, walk a few feet away, empty it on the ground and then start sifting through the contents, until he couldn't stand it anymore.

He turned off the equipment, went over to her and demanded to know what she was doing, to which she merely replied, "You do it your way, I'll do it mine."

When he resumed his seat on the bulldozer, he decided he *was* glad he didn't understand.

The desert sun was hot enough to force him to keep his shirt on to protect himself, well tanned though he was, from its harmful rays, and already he was soaked through with sweat. His hat band, too, was dark and damp, and Lyndsay wasn't faring much better.

She wore her hair pushed up beneath a Stetson much like his, but she was working in direct sunlight and her cheeks were flushed with exposure—where they were visible beneath the streaks of dirt, that was. A long-sleeved shirt protected her arms, but it was open over a T-shirt that was dark with a triangular patch of perspiration that began between her breasts and disappeared into the waistband of her shorts. Her white socks were dusty above the tops of her hiking boots, and her knees were shiny with perspiration. For some inexplicable reason Jed thought that was the sexiest thing he had ever seen.

She squatted there in the dirt, occasionally wiping her face with the back of her arm while she sorted through a pile of broken rocks and loosened dirt, squinting in the sun and intent upon her work, and Jed's eyes returned to her knees so often and with such fascination that more than once he narrowly avoided an accident. His own weakness only irritated him further.

He had spent half the night trying to figure out why she was holding back so stubbornly on the diary, when she must have known that only made him more determined to see it. And trying to figure out why her refusal should leave him feeling so betrayed.

Her siting of the tree and the stream fork had been neither coincidence nor imagination; the metal detector had proven that. Did she think he was a complete fool? She *had* to have some source of information he did not—the diary.

Then why hadn't she simply told him so? Why had she pretended to be surprised when he showed her his discovery?

More importantly, perhaps, why had she told him anything at all? Once she was inside the canyon and could get her bearings, why not just keep her information—and the treasure—for herself?

Women, he thought again in a mixture of frustration and contempt. Why couldn't they just stand up and fight like men? Why all this subterfuge and dissembling and conniving?

Of course, he was forced to admit, without it they wouldn't be women. And they wouldn't be even half as dangerous.

LYNDSAY KNEW THAT THE JOB she had assigned herself was pointless busywork, but there was too much of the archaeologist left in her to just stand by idly while tons of earth were disarranged. She had no idea what she was looking for or whether she'd even recognize it if she found it. The truth of the matter was she didn't really expect to find anything, and the way Jed was desecrating the hillside by the bulldozer-shovelful, she doubted whether he would, either. But sifting through the rubble gave her a legitimate reason to be on-site, just in case.

And it gave her an excuse to be near Jed.

There was something about men and their machines that never failed to strike a responsive chord in Lyndsay. Sweat and muscle, thundering power held effortlessly under control...oh, yes. She'd be the first to admit there was a definite appeal in the way his biceps flexed as he shifted levers, in the expression of focused attention on his face as he guided the huge machine backward and forward. So much appeal, in fact, that she found she was spending a great deal more time watching him than watching the rubble she was supposed to be studying. But that was not the reason she wanted to be out there with him.

She couldn't figure him out.

He was angry with her about something besides the diary. No, *angry* was too strong a word. Jed, like she, might have flares of temper, heated confrontations and verbal outbursts, but anger implied a sustained waste of emotion that he was too shrewd to nourish. No, what Jed Donovan was at present was extremely guarded, far more suspicious than that business over the diary could account for and as wary with her as though he expected her to literally pull a knife out of her boot and stab him in the back. She hated that.

She hated the distance that he had put between them, she hated the fact that she had probably been the cause of it and most of all she hated that she cared. At this moment she should be searching the trailer for the map—*that* was all she was interested in. Instead, she was digging through bucketfuls of broken rocks and earth for no other reason than that Jed was mad at her and she didn't want him to be.

Why did she care what Jed felt? He was nothing to her; there was nothing between them. And if she was smart, there never would be.

One thing was for certain. If she was going to start making her living through underhanded dealings such as this, she would have to learn to stop getting so attached to her victims.

Even as her eyes kept wandering repeatedly back to Jed, as her brooding thoughts were as far as they could possibly be from the job at hand, her experienced fingers were quickly and efficiently examining every lump of soil or broken rock that passed through them and making a determination by touch alone. Though it had been years since she had done this kind of work, there was a comfortable familiarity about it, and still she could do it in her sleep.

She was so distracted however, or perhaps so lulled by the routine, that when her fingers first discovered the anomaly in the handful of dirt she was sifting, she almost let it drop. Her attention snapped back not an instant too soon, and she separated the irregularly shaped stone from the others in her hand.

First of all, it wasn't a stone. That it was some kind of metal object was clear even before she started chipping away the encrustations with her fingernails, and anticipation tightened in her stomach though she couldn't determine whether it was from dread or hope. If this was what the metal detector had picked up, the search was over. If it turned out to be someone's earring or copper-filled quarter, they had torn up half the hillside for nothing. But if it was something else . . .

Lyndsay chipped away the dirt until the flat cartwheel shape became apparent. She had brought along a bucket of water, not expecting to use it but following long-ingrained habit. She dunked the artifact in the water and swished it around, watching as the years of encrusted soil washed away and the shape became clear.

But even then it was a long time before she could believe her eyes, and even longer before she could get her breath enough to whisper, "Oh my God..."

It was a gold coin.

WHEN JED SAW LYNDSAY waving her arms at him and screaming he thought she had seen a snake, or possibly even been bitten by one. He jumped off the bulldozer, leaving the engine running, and ran toward her.

He grabbed her by the shoulders and shouted, "What? Are you hurt?" before it even registered that the expression on her face was exultation, not fear.

"Look!" she cried. They both had to shout to be heard over the sound of the engine. "Look what I found!"

She held up her hand, and in it was a round, flat piece of what was unmistakably gold.

About two inches across, it was worn away at the edges in a roughly circular shape. The carving was faded beyond recognition, and if any identifying marks were left they would only be visible under a high-powered microscope. But it was definitely a coin.

Jed took the object from her hand slowly, trying not to overreact. But after fifteen years—no, after a hundred years—of searching and finding nothing, after coming to the edge of giving up over and over again, to suddenly be presented with the first concrete evidence that he might not, after all, be a complete fool . . . it was hard not to overreact.

He looked at Lyndsay and saw the joyous incredulity in her eyes, and the battle he was fighting for control was all but lost. He closed his fist around the coin, he closed his eyes. He turned a little away from her and the slow long breath he released was a fervent *"Yes!"*

It was real. After all this time, here was proof. Something solid and concrete that he could hold in his hand. *His.* It was really going to happen and it was so close he could taste it.

The silence brought him back to reality and only then did he realize how intense the emotion that seized him was. Triumph, or the mere possibility of triumph, had blotted out everything else until he opened his eyes and saw Lyndsay jumping down from the bulldozer, where she had just turned off the engine.

"We won't be using that anymore," she said. Her color was high and her eyes bright with excitement despite the forced nonchalance of her tone. "From now on it's shoveful by shoveful."

Jed wanted to make sure his voice worked before he tried to use it, so he swallowed hard. "You think the box might have broken open in one of the landslides that covered over the hiding place."

"A landslide," she agreed thoughtfully, "or even a small earthquake. Donovan, let me see it for a minute."

By that time he was able to open his hand, and release the coin. Lyndsay took it between her fingers, studying it for a minute.

"Do you know what U.S. mint looked like in the nineteenth century?"

For a moment Jed just stared at her, as surprised by the question as he was by his own answer. But at least thinking about it distracted him from the impulse to race around the canyon shouting his good fortune to the skies, and anchored him to reality again.

"No," he admitted. "Jeez, that's funny. You'd think that would be the first thing I would have checked out. God knows I've seen every other treasure exhibit in the country, but I never ran across nineteenth-century gold coins. Not that I recall, anyway."

"Me, either." Lyndsay was still looking at the coin, turning it over in her hand, watching the play of light on its dull burnished surface. "My field is a few centuries earlier. But this is awfully big, isn't it? And do you really think it would be this badly damaged after only some hundred years? I mean, you can't even read the writing."

Jed just laughed. He couldn't help it; he felt too good not to. "*That's* what I have an archaeologist along for. To tell me what I'm not seeing with my own eyes."

He gestured toward the coin. "What difference does it make how big it is or how worn it is? Gold is measured by weight and this is only one coin. There's a whole chestful of them buried in that hillside somewhere!''

Lyndsay didn't want to believe it; she tried not to believe it because only idiots and dreamers looked for pots of gold at the end of the rainbow. But there wasn't a rainbow in sight and what she held in her hand was unmistakably gold. She looked up at Jed and couldn't hold back the slow grin that spread over her face. "Yeah," she said. "There just might be.''

He laughed again and this time she laughed with him. Enthusiasm sparked in the air like a contagion, fanned and fueled by each of them to the other. Lyndsay did not know whether he made the first move or she did, but they were in each other's arms, hugging and laughing. He caught her at the waist, lifted her off her feet and whirled her around, and she squealed like a schoolgirl.

When he set her down, she staggered on her feet a little, still laughing, clinging to him for balance. She looked up at him and his eyes were dancing, his breath as uneven as hers. And slowly the laughter faded, in him as it did in her, and mutated into something more charged, deeper.

He looked at her with eyes that so effortlessly seemed to probe her soul. He said huskily, "I'm glad you're here.''

Lyndsay's breath went shallow in her throat as his hands came up to cup her face. Gently his thumbs stroked the corners of her lips, parting them. His eyes were like magnets. He bent his head, bringing his face close to hers. He prodded her mouth open with his tongue.

Lyndsay lost all strength in her knees. Everything within her seemed to swirl and melt together in a rush of heat and sensation: the taste of him, the scent, the power, the feel. She moaned in delicious helplessness, her fingers tightening on his forearms. His hat tumbled to the ground, so did hers. His hands moved down, cupping her buttocks, pushing her into him. Resistance, if ever there had been any, melted away; common sense, self-defense and will followed close after.

Crazy, she thought helplessly, wonderfully. Crazy to try to keep away from one another, crazy to set up rules they knew they were going to break, crazy to think anything in the world was more important than this moment of triumph and surrender, the wonderful, wild, ecstatic moment of shared victory and shared wonder that ended so inevitably, so perfectly, in one another's arms.

Lyndsay heard the sound behind them long before she recognized it, or even registered it; it simply wasn't relevant. All that mattered was Jed and what he was doing to her. Sensation mushroomed, will was swept away—she was drowning in his arms. And then, when she couldn't tell where her body ended and his began, when she was beginning to feel her entire sense of self sink into him helplessly, wonderfully, his muscles seemed to stiffen. His hands moved up to her waist and remained there to steady her as, incredibly, he moved away.

Then Lyndsay noticed what Jed must have noticed much sooner. A voice that was not Jed's said, "Pardon me."

Lyndsay whirled around, stumbling a little with the suddenness of the movement. Jed's hand steadied her.

"Gabe," he said. His voice sounded strained and his breathing uneven.

Gabe Blackwater smiled, his eyes twinkling in a friendly way. "I hope I haven't come calling at an inconvenient time."

"I've got to say," Jed answered, bending to pick up his hat, "I have been happier to see you."

Gabe nodded toward the now-silent bulldozer. "I heard the equipment and got curious," he admitted, and he smiled at Lyndsay. "Although I did have ulterior—or maybe I should say alternative—motive for coming over. Mary sent me with an invitation to supper, if you don't have any plans."

It was impossible not to return his smile, despite her embarrassment and discomfiture. She managed to bring her breathing under control well enough to reply with a fair imitation of lightness. "I'll have to check my calendar, but I think you're in luck."

Gabe's eyes twinkled with the deepening of his smile and Lyndsay relaxed almost against her will. He had a way of immediately putting a person at ease, like a kindly grandfather or a favorite uncle.

He turned to Jed in the same easy conversational way. "So, how goes it?"

Jed hesitated for less than half a breath. "Actually," he said, "it looks like we might be having some luck."

And before Lyndsay could guess what he was about to do, much less object, he had taken the coin from her hand and passed it to Gabe.

Gabe examined the coin with interest, and perhaps the strangest thing about the whole affair was that, from that point on, it seemed perfectly natural to Lyndsay that he should do so. Under ordinary circumstances she never would have trusted a stranger with their discovery; it was tantamount to putting up a flashing arrow with a neon sign that said Treasure Hidden Here. She did not think that Jed was in the habit of sharing everything he knew with anyone who happened by, either. But with Gabe it seemed . . . well, perfectly all right.

He turned the coin over in his hand. "It's old," he said.

"Over a hundred years," agreed Jed.

Gabe shook his head thoughtfully. "Older."

The word made Lyndsay's pulse stutter with surprise, then pick up its pace. And when his eyes met hers she knew he was thinking exactly what she had been.

"Spanish?" she said.

"Maybe." He returned the coin to her. "Maybe even older. Whatever it is, though, I think you're probably right—it's not the only one of its kind. You've got to be getting close.''

''That's exactly what we thought,'' Jed said with satisfaction.

Gabe nodded toward the hillside. ''Looks like you've got your work cut out for you. It's got to be shovels and pickaxes from now on. You need any help, you let me know.''

''Thanks, Gabe.''

Gabe smiled once more at Lyndsay. ''Mary says you come on over about sundown. Be sure to bring a flashlight for the walk back.''

''Thanks, Gabe. We'll be there.''

He started back toward his own camp, waving over his shoulder. ''Don't work too hard in the heat of the day.''

Lyndsay was still examining the coin in her hand, frowning a little. Jed looked back at her, following the direction of her gaze.

''Older than Spanish?'' he inquired. ''What do you think he meant by that? I thought the Spanish were the first explorers to pass through this part of the country.''

Lyndsay had to clear her throat before she could speak. ''Some people think there were civilizations who had risen and fallen long before the first Europeans ever set foot in this country, before the Spanish ever thought of exploring it.'' Her voice grew softer, more distracted, as she added, ''Mighty civilizations, magical and mystical and full of mysteries we couldn't even begin to comprehend, even now. My father was one of those people.''

Her hand closed convulsively around the coin and she finished flatly, ''Another one of his theories that did not receive a particularly warm reception. He was practically laughed out of the business, as a matter of fact.''

The confession embarrassed her, as references to her father's follies often did, and she looked up at Jed. His gaze was sober and sympathetic, containing none of the amusement she had expected to find there. The memory of what Gabe's visit had interrupted seemed to swell between them. Lyndsay's heartbeat grew congested in her chest, and she suddenly felt awkward.

''Well,'' she said. She offered the coin to him. ''I guess this is yours.''

He made no move to take it, and his expression was unchanging. ''No, you found it.''

Another heartbeat of silence, and two. Had their former passion been a momentary aberration or a fundamental change in their relationship? Would he now suggest they pick up where they had left off before Gabe interrupted, or would he pretend nothing had ever happened?

What was the most compelling to him—Lyndsay, or the treasure?

Lyndsay wasn't sure she could have answered that question had their positions been reversed, and she wasn't even completely sure what she was hoping for.

All she knew was that she wanted him to take her in his arms. She wanted to recapture that moment of shared, explosive joy and she wanted to let it grow and crest and take them where it would. She wanted Jed to want it, too.

The silence spun out between them, measured in heartbeats and expectation. It was almost a relief to have an end to the tension when he spoke, although what he said was not exactly what she expected to hear.

"Well," he said, glancing away somewhat uncomfortably, "like the man said, we've got our work cut out for us the rest of the day. Better get started."

After a moment Lyndsay managed a tight smile, tucked the coin into her pocket and walked with him to get the shovels and picks.

Chapter Twelve

Lyndsay was alone in the trailer.

They had returned from the site a while ago and she had taken a shower. Now Jed had left her to dress while he went outside to shower and change.

This was the perfect time to search for the map. She was surprised by how long it took for her to realize that. Chances were he had simply returned the map to the ceiling, never thinking she'd be so obvious as to try to remove it.

All she had to do was climb on the bed, and push out the panel, remove the map and stuff it into her duffel bag. Tonight when he was asleep, she would slip quietly away and that would be that.

She stood in the middle of the room, staring at the ceiling. Thirty, forty seconds tops. She could do it. This might be her last chance.

She took a step toward the bed, then stopped. She looked at the ceiling panel again, then turned away and sat down at the desk, where she picked up her cosmetic bag and began to put on her makeup.

She told herself she didn't have enough time, but that wasn't the real reason. The truth was that there was a little voice in the back of her mind, whispering how foolish it would be to settle for the map when the treasure was so close. And she listened to it.

That was the first time in her life she had ever chosen the birds in the bush over the one in her hand. It was, of course, the kind of thing her father had done constantly.

Jed returned in clean jeans and a long-sleeved denim shirt, freshly shaved, hair towel-dried and tousled, smelling like spicy soap and looking good enough to make Lyndsay's knees weak. She wished absurdly that she had a pretty dress to put on.

She had to settle for jeans and a sweater against the evening's expected chill, and, because it was late and Jed was impatient, she slicked her wet hair back and tied it in a ponytail.

"If I get pneumonia, it'll be your fault," she complained as they set off across the canyon. "How far is it to his camp, anyway?"

"About half a mile."

Lyndsay groaned. "We couldn't have taken the truck?"

"You'll be glad of the exercise after one of Mary's meals."

"This better be good," she muttered.

A few steps later they picked up the scent of something delicious cooking over a mesquite-wood fire, and her grumpiness started to fade. The closer they got, the better it smelled, and appetite pushed aside fatigue as they let the scent guide them to the camp.

Lyndsay had expected a campsite much like their own, with perhaps a late-model RV instead of a battered trailer, for Gabe Blackwater struck her as a somewhat well-to-do retired gentleman with the means to spend his leisure years seeing America in style. She was surprised to see a *real* campsite: open fire, a double tent, even a smoke pit. It was from the latter that the most succulent scents emanated, and Lyndsay's stomach growled in anticipation.

Gabe waved and called a greeting when he saw them, ushering them over to the fire enthusiastically. He was wearing a Hawaiian print shirt, khaki trousers and calfskin moccasins; his face was wreathed in smiles. He was the perfect portrait of the genial neighbor hosting a backyard barbecue.

"Welcome, welcome," he said warmly, drawing them in. "And right on time. Lyndsay, don't you look lovely? Come meet my wife, Mary."

Mary was a square-faced, stout woman of indeterminate age whose jet-black hair was worn in two shoulder-length pigtails and whose immobile expression defined *inscrutable*. She wore a shapeless flowered smock and sandals, and she acknowledged her husband's introduction without smiling.

"Something smells absolutely wonderful," Lyndsay enthused.

"Oh, Mary's this century's greatest cook, all right," Gabe agreed. "She makes the best campfire biscuits in three states, you can ask anybody."

Mary lifted the lid on a large Dutch oven nestled in the coals of the smoke pit with no visible signs of gratification. She stirred the contents silently, and the odors wafting from the pot made Lyndsay light-headed.

"Is there anything I can do to help?" Lyndsay offered.

Without giving his wife a chance to reply, Gabe draped his arm around Lyndsay's shoulders and led her away. "You're a guest," he insisted. "We're not going to put you to work just yet! Besides, I wouldn't want to deprive myself of your company. Tell me how the day's work has gone."

Before she knew it, Lyndsay was talking to him as though he were her oldest friend. They drew up canvas chairs around the fire and Gabe served them homebrew out of an old-fashioned clay jug—a rich sweet fruity concoction that went straight to Lyndsay's head and flowed like molten honey through her veins. In no time at all she was having a wonderful time.

Throughout the evening Mary never said a word. It might have been the homebrew, it might have been Gabe's and Jed's casual attitude toward the taciturn wife, but after a time, Lyndsay ceased to find this strange. And when she tasted the ambrosia that Mary dished up from the Dutch oven she couldn't have cared if it had been cooked by Attila the Hun.

The dish resembled a shepherd's pie, with succulent morsels of meat and vegetables slow-cooked and faintly flavored with woodsmoke, wild herbs and perhaps just the faintest hint of wine. Served with it were biscuits the size of teacups and so fluffy they crumbled in the fingers almost before they reached the mouth. There was plenty of the sweet heady wine and a buttery, crusty fruit cobbler for dessert.

The daylight faded and the dancing flames of the fire provided shadowy, romantic illumination. There was laughter and easy conversation, but Lyndsay did not remember anything in particular that was said. What she did remember was how Jed's face looked in the firelight, rugged and strong, like an old-time cowboy, how his eyes crinkled when he laughed, how pleasant it was to see him relaxed and at ease with his friends and how good it felt just to be with him.

As the night deepened, a chill filled the air and Lyndsay was glad of her sweater. Mary served a dark sweet coffee that could have surpassed anything offered by a gourmet coffee house. Jed sat on the ground feeding sticks into the fire as he sipped his coffee, and after a while Lyndsay sat beside him. The flames warmed her face as the cup warmed her hands. Her shoulder brushed against Jed's and he looked at her. His smile warmed the rest of her as she settled beside him, close enough to touch at more than one point. He tossed the last stick into the fire and curved his hand around her waist comfortably, sipping his coffee.

Gabe lit a pipe, and the fragrant aroma of rich tobacco further scented the air. "I understand your father was interested in the Anasazi," he said to Lyndsay.

She was a little surprised. "Why, yes."

He nodded thoughtfully. "Interesting course of study. Many people believe that they were the great superrace from which all the tribes are descended. This part of the country is filled with legends of the Old Ones. Many say this—" and he gestured with his pipe to indicate the entire canyon "—is their holy ground."

Something in his words struck a chord of uneasiness within Lyndsay, or perhaps it was the sudden gust of a cool breeze that brushed the back of her neck. A shiver went down her spine.

She tried to chase away the disquiet with lightness. "I heard it was haunted. Ever seen any ghosts?"

His eyes twinkled in the dark. "This canyon is filled with them."

"Do you think the Anasazi were here?" Lyndsay asked, and his opinion really seemed to matter.

The effects of the wine were still very much in evidence and she did not think the coffee was completely undiluted, either, which might have explained the distinctly peculiar turn the conversation had taken. Or perhaps that was just another facet of the very strange evening.

"I don't know," he answered seriously. "I don't know if that's even their proper name. But in almost every Native American culture there is reference to another people, an ancient people who held miraculous powers and all-lost wisdom, and who are in one way or another responsible for our being here. Some even speculate that this same superrace predates the ancient Mayan and in fact might even be their ancestors. And what I find really interesting is that this canyon, this 'holy ground' has always been known to every tribe—but no one tribe ever claimed it."

Lyndsay frowned a little with the effort to concentrate. Jed's hand was moving in a slow and absent caress up and down her spine, which made the task much more difficult.

"You talk like an anthropologist," she said.

He chuckled. "Just a student of history—tribal and otherwise."

"What tribe are you from?"

He chewed on his pipe and seemed not to have heard. "You know," he said thoughtfully, "if there is any evidence of the Anasazi—or anyone else—in this canyon, I have a feeling you'll be the one to uncover it." And he smiled. "That would be something, wouldn't it? If the daughter were to prove the father's theories after his death and bring honor to his name?"

Lyndsay returned his smile. "I'm afraid it would take more than that to bring honor to my father's name." But she thought it was a sweet thing for him to have said anyway.

After that, the conversation turned to archaeology and anthropology and ghost stories and sunken galleons and astronomy and even touched, even Lyndsay recalled correctly, on ancient astronauts. Gabe was articulate and entertaining, and although he seemed to know a little bit about almost everything, Lyndsay noticed that he invariably managed to avoid revealing anything at all about himself.

The embers of the fire had died down by the time they left and Lyndsay was amazed how quickly the evening had passed. She was sincere when she told Gabe what an enjoyable time she had had, and effusively thanked Mary for the meal. Mary didn't say a word.

The sky was brilliant with stars and the moon bright enough to cast bluish shadows along the canyon floor as they walked back to their own camp. Jed carried a flashlight, but didn't turn it on. His arm was around her waist, presumably to keep her from stumbling in the dark, and Lyndsay walked with her fingers tucked into his back belt loop.

Perhaps it was that comfortable closeness between them, the lowering of barriers that seemed so natural and right; perhaps it was the good meal and stimulating conversation and the campfire and the cool desert air that was so reminiscent of pleasant days of her youth; perhaps it was the midnight blue sky and the Christmas-bright stars and the vast peace and silence of the land around them, but the night had a magical, ethereal quality that seemed to go on forever.

Lyndsay tilted her head back and almost got dizzy looking at the stars. "Just look at that," she murmured. "What a night, huh?"

He agreed that it was indeed.

"That Gabe is quite a character. Do *you* know what tribe he's from?"

Jed hesitated. "I don't think he ever said. I assume Ute."

"And Mary. *Can* she speak, do you think?"

"She never has."

Lyndsay was thoughtful for a moment. "Do you think he put something in the wine?"

Jed chuckled. "A few peyote buttons, a little mescaline? I wouldn't put it past the old buzzard. Why, do you feel it?"

"A little." She glanced up at him. His face was beautiful in the moonlight. "You?"

"Yeah," he admitted. "A little." And he smiled at her, his hand caressing her waist. "Or it could be the company."

Lyndsay thought, from her point of view, it most definitely was the company. Just being near him had been making her high from the moment they met.

She chuckled softly. "Maybe it was an aphrodisiac he put in the wine."

She could feel his smile penetrate every cell in her skin, and the husky quality of his voice traveled like an electric current down her spinal cord. "I think an aphrodisiac is the last thing either one of us needs."

She said a little breathlessly, "I agree."

"Of course we have a deal."

It sounded a little like a question and Lyndsay knew the answer she should give. She couldn't bring herself to do so, and said nothing. They walked in magically charged silence for a while.

Then Jed said, "Did it bother you, what he said about your father?"

She glanced at him, surprised. "No. Why?"

"No reason. You just seemed to be a little touchy on that subject."

"I guess I am. With pretty good reason."

"Odd that Gabe should know about him, though," Jed said thoughtfully.

Lyndsay stared at him. "You mean you didn't tell him?"

Jed merely shook his head.

"That *is* weird," Lyndsay muttered, and puzzling over it kept her preoccupied—that, and the caress of Jed's hand on her waist, the brush of his hip against hers—the rest of the way back to their camp.

They had left no lights on in the trailer and it had an abandoned, ghostly aura to it. In fact, tonight of all nights Lyndsay could have believed the canyon was haunted. Gabe *must* have put something in the wine, she decided.

Jed's hand dropped from her waist as they reached the trailer. "You're probably tired," he said. "You should turn in."

Lyndsay knew she should be tired, but with all that had happened today it was going to be hard to wind down. But she also knew the dangers of lingering with Jed in the dark.

"Yeah," she said. "You too."

"I don't know. I might sit up awhile, look at the stars. It's a nice night."

She felt like a teenager on her first date, lingering at the door to say good-night. Not certain what she was waiting for, wondering whether she should say good-night at all . . . which was ridiculous.

Of course she should say good-night. She had no choice. She had made the rules and that was perhaps the only honest thing she had done since meeting Jed. She couldn't keep playing a game she had no intention of finishing, getting more and more involved with him when she knew in the end her only intention was to stab him in the back and walk away.

Wasn't it?

She was amazed at how hard it was to say, "Good night, Donovan. I had a really nice time tonight."

He smiled, acknowledging the absurdity of the formality. "I'll call you sometime."

Lyndsay managed to return his smile, and then she went inside. Alone.

Chapter Thirteen

She undressed in the dark and pulled on a T-shirt for sleeping. But once in bed she didn't even pretend to sleep. She sat with her knees drawn up and a pillow propped behind her shoulders, wondering how she had made such a mess out of things.

It all would have been so much easier if Jed Donovan hadn't been so...well, so *him*. If he hadn't been quite so tall, if he walked with a little less of a swagger, if those green eyes had been just a little less shrewd... If he had been dull or stupid or cruel or uneducated or clumsy. If he had been anyone in the world except the only man she had ever met that she both liked and respected, the first man who could actually outthink her and who was unsurprised by what he concluded when he did, the man who could make her muscles melt with his touch and her heart pound with his gaze... If he hadn't been so damn near perfect, her choices would be so much easier now.

Jed was the only man she had ever known who did not need her more than she needed him, the only man she didn't feel compelled to take care of. From her father to her lovers, the men in her life had invariably been little boys in disguise, looking to her for nurturing and protection. But Jed ... how many more times could she expect a man like him to come along?

How many men like him were left?

She couldn't stay cramped up in the trailer when her head was spinning in circles and nervous energy was pulsing in her veins. She flung the sheet aside and got out of bed, thrusting her feet into a pair of battered sneakers. She opened the door quietly, so as not to disturb Jed if he had already gone to sleep, and stepped outside.

He hadn't gone to sleep, and Lyndsay didn't even try to pretend to herself that she wasn't glad.

He had taken his sleeping bag from the folding cot and opened it on the ground. He sat there, with one arm propped on his upraised knee, gazing out across the moonlit canyon. He glanced around at her approach.

"Mind some company?" Lyndsay said, feeling suddenly shy and a little like an intruder.

"Help yourself." He patted the open sleeping bag.

Lyndsay sat down, near him but not too close, and shared his view. The silence was comfortable between them, but just as comfortable to break.

"What are you thinking about?"

He gave a soft grunt of laughter. "Well, let's see. Today I found a gold coin that's going to lead me to a treasure that's been lost for over a hundred years. What do you think I'm thinking about?"

"What to wear at your press conference?"

He gave her a measuring look in the dark. "You're a funny lady," he said. "You invited yourself along on this dig, you spent an entire day in the broiling sun sifting through rock and dirt—you're the one who found the coin in the first place. But every time I mention the treasure, you stiffen up, like it's a joke in bad taste."

She couldn't meet his eyes. "I do not."

"Trust me," he responded mildly. "There's not a whole lot in this world I consider myself an expert on, but a woman's body language—that I know."

Lyndsay found a twig on the ground outside the square of the sleeping bag; she picked it up and absently began to stab at the sand with it.

"It's hard for me, Donovan," she said, her tone slightly muffled. "All my life I listened to my father with his improbable tales, his wild theories, his crazy dreams... And every time he was so *sure*, so convincing. This treasure... it's a million-to-one shot—you know that. Even Gabe didn't think that coin looked like anything that ever came out of the U.S. treasury. Who knows where it came from? Maybe some Indian tribe buried coins with their dead; a lot of cultures did, and this is supposed to be holy ground, isn't it? It might not have anything to do with the treasure at all.''

''There's something in that hillside,'' Jed said. And she had no argument for that.

Lyndsay drew in a long slow breath and released it shallowly. She pulled up her knees and encircled them with her arm, stretching the T-shirt over them. She did not know why the confession was so hard to make, but it was.

''Lost treasure, cryptic maps... God, it just sounds so *crazy*. I know you believe it, Donovan, and you've got good reason,'' she added with a quick glance at him. ''And God knows treasure has been found before. But you've got to understand, the kind of people my father attracted, the life he led—crazies and dreamers everywhere, and I learned to be skeptical real fast. This whole thing—well, it reminds me of Icarus, chasing the sun.''

''Icarus,'' he repeated. ''The Greek dude with the wax wings?''

Lyndsay's lips tightened wryly. ''That's right. And you remember what happened when he got too close to the sun.''

''Not exactly a three-point landing,'' he agreed. ''Fortunately, technology has come a long way since then, and I know a hell of a lot more about flying than he did.''

Lyndsay laughed softly, giving a gentle shake of her head. ''You really are stubborn, aren't you?''

"If I weren't, I would've given this up a long time ago. And as far as I can see, a little sun-chasing never hurt anybody."

Lyndsay dropped her gaze to the series of perforations she had made with the stick in the moonlit sand. Her voice was muffled. "Sometimes I wish I could be like that. Believe in crazy dreams. But I can't."

"Maybe you just never had a dream worth believing in."

The cast of her smile was a little bitter, and she was glad he couldn't see it in the dark. "Maybe I've just spent too much of my life picking up the mess other people's dreams made when they fell apart."

Jed was silent for a moment. He wondered if she had any idea what she looked like, sitting there with her knees drawn up beneath the T-shirt, her hair cascading in moon-touched waves over her shoulders, poking holes in the ground with a stick and talking about lost dreams. Strong, competent, take-charge Lyndsay Blake. Always in control, never wrong, never willing to back down. Looking at her now, all he wanted to do was draw her head on his shoulder and promise her a dream that no one would steal.

Damn, how had he ever gotten involved with such a woman? And what in God's name was he supposed to do about it now?

"Hey," he said. And she glanced up at him, pushing back the veil of her hair. Yearning went through Jed like a sweet summer's breeze.

"You never did tell me," he said.

"Tell you what?"

"What you're going to do with your part of the treasure."

She looked uncomfortable and embarrassed. "Come on, Donovan. I just told you—I'm not the kind to count chickens before they're hatched."

"No, you come on. Lighten up. Play the game. What would you do with a million dollars?"

Much against her will, Lyndsay's lips tightened with a smile. "A million and a quarter," she corrected.

He waited.

After a moment Lyndsay tossed the stick away and glanced at him with a half-smothered grin. She knew exactly what he was trying to do and it was, as he knew very well, irresistible. She adored him for that.

She encircled her knees with her arms again, gazing up at the canopy of stars that seemed to have grown even brighter and more majestic since the last time she had looked. "That's easy," she said. "The first thing I'd do if I had that kind of money would be to go to Cairo. Every archaeologist worth his salt has been to Egypt." She gave a small, slightly uncomfortable shrug. "My father used to talk about it a lot. He always expected that I would go, be involved in some important dig.... I couldn't explain to him, of course, that the reason I would *never* be invited on an Egyptian dig was because of him, and the reputation he'd built that had filtered down on to me.''

Jed's silence was gentle and understanding, but it did not last long enough to become uncomfortable.

''I don't know. A million dollars to dig in the dirt? You can do that and be poor.''

She laughed. ''I guess I could, if I had any interest at all in digging in the dirt. I don't want to go to Egypt to work. I just want to go to Egypt. To have a drink atop the pyramid at Giza, to sail into the port at sunset—in my own private yacht, of course—to cruise the Nile on a painted barge...''

Jed grinned. ''*Now* you're dreaming.''

Lyndsay shifted her gaze to him. ''What about you? You never answered the question, either.''

He leaned back on one elbow, and his expression grew thoughtful as he gazed out over the desert. ''That's probably because I didn't know the answer. I mean, I've been sitting here thinking about just that, and it occurred to me that I've spent my whole life looking for the treasure without once asking myself what I'd do with it if I had it.''

He shot a rueful glance at her. ''Kind of like old Mr. Wax Wings, huh? I wonder what *he* thought he'd do with the sun if he reached it.''

He shrugged. ''You talk about your crazies and your dreamers... It's been passed down in my family for generations. In a way, it's almost like the searching was more important than the finding. My grandfather was the one who always preached that the money belonged to the tribe. My father talked about building a children's hospital on the reservation. If you want to know the truth, I just never thought I'd get this close.''

He looked at her, his eyes as soft as jewels in the night. ''And I wouldn't have, if it hadn't been for you.''

Great, Lyndsay thought, and she shifted her gaze away from his. *Not only am I stealing from a man I might very well be falling in love with, now I'm stealing from sick children.* But she knew the decision had really been made much earlier, for it came to her with far too much ease.

She just wasn't cut out for this. She never had been.

She stood up. ''Excuse me a minute. I'll be right back.''

Jed sat up, puzzled, and watched her go into the trailer. She returned a moment later with something in her hand.

Lyndsay dropped it into his lap. The diary. The lock was open, the clasp undone. Jed looked at her questioningly, but she stood over him, stiff and uncommunicative. He opened the diary.

He turned the first page, the next. He began to thumb through more rapidly. Page after page of scrawled columns, names, numbers...

It seemed to Jed that time stood still while he turned the pages, stared at the lines without reading them, without comprehending them, trying to make himself see what simply wasn't there. And then, just as slowly, understanding dawned; still he couldn't quite believe it.

He looked up at her. His voice was oddly flat. "An address book?"

She nodded miserably, dropping to the ground beside him. "I knew you'd be looking for something, and that was the only thing I had that looked like a diary. I thought it would stall you until . . . well, until I could get the map."

Again time stretched out in long, echoing beats. Jed waited for the anger, the incredulity, the sense of betrayal. All he felt, in fact, was curiosity.

He dropped his gaze back to the book in his hand. "But—I don't understand. This doesn't make any sense."

"Oh, Donovan." She pushed her hand through her hair, her voice heavy with defeat. "There isn't any diary. There never was. My father never wrote anything down and he forgot his 'visions' or whatever they were the minute they were over. As for that newspaper clipping of yours—hell, he spent the last five years of his life dousing for water for whatever people would pay him, and if he ever was in this part of the country, that was probably what he was doing. He never said anything about 'untold wealth.'"

She had to stop for breath, and then she plunged on. There was no point in holding anything back now. "The only reason I came out here with you was to get that map. I've already had an offer for it, but I guess you already figured that out. I was going to share the money with you," she added. Then she felt compelled to admit, "Well, maybe not fifty-fifty but I would have shared."

Throughout her confession Jed had not made a sound, nor even looked up from the address book, whose pages he turned with slow, methodical motions. Lyndsay didn't know what else to say, except to add lowly, "I guess you'll want me to leave in the morning. Maybe Gabe can take me back. I won't tell anyone—" she gestured toward the canyon "—about this."

She turned and started back toward the trailer, knowing that if she stayed another moment, if Jed even once raised his eyes to her and she saw the hurt and betrayal there, her carefully pasted together emotions would shatter into a thousand fragments and nothing would ever put her back together again.

"Why?"

The word, simple and quietly spoken, went through her like a knife. She stopped in place, bracing herself against the pain.

"Why go through all this? Why the elaborate lies? Why work so hard to keep me in the dark?"

There was no accusation in his tone, just genuine curiosity. Nonetheless, the guilt, the shame and the remorse welled up inside Lyndsay until she thought she would choke on them. She couldn't turn around to face him, but she couldn't refuse to answer, either. He deserved that much.

"Oh, Jed." Her voice was tight and she struggled to keep it steady. "You are looking at one screwed-up person. At first—I knew it was the only way to keep you interested enough to take me along. Later...I wanted to tell you the truth. I knew you needed to know and I hated keeping it from you...but you see, by then I'd started to fall in love with you and the lie...was my only defense. The only thing that I could keep between us."

She heard him rise and come to stand behind her, close but not touching. "Are you in love with me, Lyndsay?" he inquired softly.

Lyndsay tilted her head back toward the stars that were suddenly blurred by a mist of tears, and drew a deep breath. "Yes," she whispered. Every fiber of her being ached with his nearness, with yearning and loss. "And it scares the hell out of me."

He touched her shoulder. The warmth of his hand, the gentle strength of the caress, sent a shiver of longing through her. "I'm glad you're in love with me," he said huskily. "Because I've been in love with you for quite a while now."

At first the words didn't register. When at last she understood, the wonder was mitigated by disbelief. She turned slowly to look at him, a cautious joy spiraling through her, but he raised his hand as though to ward off her embrace. And the sorrow on his face sent a chill through her.

"It's too late, isn't it?" she said hoarsely. "You can't forgive me for what I've done."

Jed shook his head slowly. "What you did was no worse than what I did. And I think you need to hear that now."

His expression was sober and pained, but he held her gaze. "I knew you were going to try to steal the map. The only reason I brought you out here was so that I would have a chance to look at the diary. I would've made sure, though, that we didn't find anything while you were here. Then when you gave up and went away..." His elaborate shrug finished the sentence.

Lyndsay knew she should be shocked, even hurt. But how could she sit in judgment on him after what she had done—or tried to do? It was hard to feel anything at all through her own tumult of emotions—of regret, anxiety, hope and confusion. He said he loved her and that was all that mattered. Yet she had betrayed him—just as he would have betrayed her if he had had a chance. How were each of them supposed to feel now?

It was a long time before either of them spoke. Then Lyndsay said quietly, "We're quite a pair."

"Yes," he agreed heavily. "We are."

He closed the book and set it carefully on the ground beside him, just as if it really were a valuable journal that held the key to a fortune, instead of a twenty-year-old collection of names and addresses she hardly ever used anymore.

"I'd give anything to do it over again, Donovan," she said huskily. "Anything."

"Yeah, me, too." Lyndsay strained to see his expression in the dark, but could find nothing in his eyes except mild curiosity. "Why tell me now?"

She tried to force a smile. "Well. The bad news is I don't make a very good crook. And that *is* bad news when you consider the kind of luck I've had trying to make a living on the right side of the law."

But the levity faded as she looked at him, and she saw no choice but honesty. She had, after all, gone this far; she might as well go all the way.

"I never met a man I admired as much as you, Donovan. Or liked. I never expected to get so attached to you." She dropped her eyes. "I just wish . . . we'd met differently."

Nothing could have surprised her more than to feel, after a moment, the gentle touch of his hand on the side of her face. She lifted her eyes slowly, and he was smiling.

"A hell of a lot about this doesn't make sense," he said, "but one thing is pretty clear in my head. I'm not sorry I met you. For one thing, whether you meant to or not, because of you I'm closer to the treasure than I've ever been in my life. For another . . ." His thumb lightly stroked her cheekbone. "I'm starting to get kind of attached to you, too."

For an endless suspended moment she looked at him, hardly daring to believe her ears, half afraid that if she so much as breathed, it would all disappear like mist on the wind. But the smile in his eyes remained steady, the caress of his hand warm, and she flowed into his embrace as naturally, as inevitably, as a stream is drawn into the river.

The kiss was at first exploratory, gentle, almost tremulous in its care, as though each of them were afraid to push the bounds of their new relationship too far, to ask too much or reveal too much. But passion swelled with a will of its own, certain, demanding, slow and thorough. They sank together to the ground, kneeling in an embrace.

Jed moved his mouth away from hers. "I do love you, Lyns," he whispered. "For whatever it's worth, I do...."

"It's worth everything." And she was lost in his kiss again, awash in need and drowning in wonder.

Lyndsay moved one leg over his, pushing herself close to him, then she was sitting astride his lap. She was naked beneath her T-shirt and she could feel his heat and hardness through his jeans.

His mouth left hers to caress her face, his breath heating and drying the moist trail left by his tongue. His hands cupped her head, fingers threaded beneath her hair. She drank him in—his breath, his touch, his heat.

He moved his face a little away, the better to look at her. "I want you," he said huskily. "I guess that's no secret. But not just sex, Lyns. *You*. Sometimes it's like a hunger inside me that I can't ever fill, and I've never felt that way about a woman before. Do you know how dangerous that is?''

''Yes,'' she whispered. Her hands moved over his chest, unfastening buttons, pushing the material aside. ''I feel the same way. It scares me sometimes.''

''We could be so bad for each other.''

''Or so good.''

Their mouths brushed, and caressed. Lyndsay unsnapped his jeans. ''Do you think it's the wine?'' she whispered.

And he breathed, ''No.''

He lifted his hips and pushed the jeans down. Lyndsay settled against him, felt him poised and strong. A slow, long sliding movement and he was inside her, filling her. Lyndsay closed her eyes and let the sensation swell through every pore, growing weak with it, losing herself in it. Losing herself in him.

Jed touched her eyelids with his thumbs. ''Look at me,'' he commanded softly.

Lyndsay opened her eyes. His face was the most beautiful thing she had ever seen.

''I'm not sorry,'' he said. ''I'm not sorry we met.''

Lyndsay lifted her hands to smooth back his hair, and the sweetness of wonder and poignancy that flooded her chest felt like tears. *Don't let me be wrong,* she thought. *Please, don't let me be wrong about this man....*

Their arms tightened around each other. They rocked each other.

A LONG TIME LATER, as they lay curled in each other's arms, sheltered by a fold of the sleeping bag against the evening's chill, Jed ran his fingers through Lyndsay's tangled hair. "Lyndsay? You awake?"

She made a contented sound against the crook of his arm and snuggled closer. For a moment what he wanted to say didn't seem quite so important anymore.

"Lyndsay, listen. I want to ask you something."

She shifted a little in his arms, opening her eyes. "Okay."

"You're telling me the truth about your father," he said carefully, studying her face. Love sated, drowsy, content. Beautiful. "There never was a diary and he never told you anything about this place."

She frowned a little, trying to follow him. "Of course I'm telling the truth."

"Then how did you know about Whispering Rock?"

"What?"

"The first day I met you. You told me about Whispering Rock. Nobody living knows what the third landmark was. How did you?"

She didn't even waste time pondering the question. She dismissed it with a simple "I made it up."

It took Jed a moment to absorb that, but even when the implication became clear, he decided to leave it for the moment.

"Okay," he said slowly, "but what about yesterday? You gave me the landmarks I needed to find the coordinates to dig. You *knew* where the treasure was."

"We haven't found any treasure yet." She sounded sleepy and disinterested.

"But the tree, the stream fork—how did you know where they used to be?"

"I told you," she murmured, yawning, "I saw them. Or thought I did."

"But they weren't really there."

"Right." Her eyes drifted closed.

"Lyndsay..." He chose his words very carefully, not even sure if he knew what it was he wanted to say. "Don't you think there's something a little strange about all this?"

Her only reply was a murmured "Hmm." She turned her face against his arm, her breathing slow and even. She was asleep.

Jed tucked the corner of the sleeping bag more securely around her, and brushed the hair away from her face. He lay awake for a long time, watching her sleep, and wondering if the woman he held in his arms might be even more precious than he knew.

LYNDSAY STOOD at the top of the rise and watched as the columns of bronze-shouldered men moved through the valley toward the tunnel, bearing chests on poles between them, dragging covered sleds. Inside those chests, upon those sleds, were all they treasured as a people—their history, their art, their cumulative knowledge. To preserve the future, they must now seal away the memories of the past.

The tunnel was the work of their most gifted designers, their most dedicated craftsmen. It would endure as long as the planet lived, a vast underground network of interlocking chambers and self-sealing rooms. Generations would be required to even map the tunnel, much less catalog the treasure that was hidden inside. That was, of course, what the designers intended, for too much knowledge too soon was a dangerous thing.

They would never return to this valley, they knew that. What was even now so carefully being sealed away inside the earth was their legacy to their children.

One chest remained to be carried away. It was open on the ground at her feet. Inside was the stuff of her lover's craft: the smooth blocks of gold and silver, the finely cut stones, the delicately wrought chains and mountings and intricately carved medallions. She knelt and placed one last item atop the others— a braided set of interlocked bracelets worked in silver and gold. As she watched, a bright tear fell and glittered on the bracelet, then melted away. It was her own.

LYNDSAY AWOKE with a start, surprised and somewhat embarrassed to find her face wet with tears.
Jed's arms were warm around her, his legs holding
and sheltering her; within the embrace of her lover
she was protected and secure. In all her life she had
never known anything more wondrous than what she
and Jed had shared tonight. Then why was she cry-
ing?

She sat up, trying not to disturb him, and reached
for her shoes. Jed stirred and murmured, "Where're
you going?"

"To the bathroom," she whispered. "Go back to
sleep."

"Are you cold? Do you want to go inside?"

She blotted the dampness from her face, leaned
over and kissed his hair. "No, it's almost morning.
I'll be back."

"Hurry," he murmured. And he was asleep again.

But when Lyndsay stepped out of the trailer again,
she didn't immediately return to the sleeping bag,
though the allure was strong. Remnants of the disturbing dream still lingered with her and she walked
a little away from the campsite, hoping the cool fresh
air would clear her mind.

It was almost dawn. The sky was a deep gray-
lavender, and all but a few of the brightest stars had
faded. Black pockets of shadow lay like sink holes
across the canyon, and Lyndsay couldn't help wondering whether one of those shadows might hide the
entrance to a secret cave, or even a tunnel. . . .

"You dream about them, too."

Lyndsay gasped at the sound of a male voice behind her, whirling around so rapidly that she almost tripped backward. Gabe Blackwater stood a little away, smiling at her in a friendly fashion.

"Good Lord!" she exclaimed, pressing her hand to her still-pounding heart. "You scared me to death."

"I didn't mean to." His easy, relaxed smile didn't fade, and he stood with his fingers tucked into his front pockets, looking out over the desert.

"Such a fascinating race," he went on, as though continuing a conversation Lyndsay could not remember beginning. "Some people believe they were incredibly advanced technologically, keepers of all the world's lost knowledge, and perhaps they're right. I see no evidence of that myself. I do believe they were extraordinary craftsmen and artisans, and that they had a highly developed social conscience in that they made sure to provide for those who came after them. Or perhaps they simply wanted to be remembered for their art, not their technology. A truly advanced civilization might make that decision, don't you think?"

Lyndsay stared across the gray expanse of early dawn that separated them, washed by a sudden chill. She said, hoarsely, "What are you talking about?"

He seemed not to have heard her. "Where did they go?" he mused. "Why did they disappear so suddenly, leaving nothing but legends in their wake? One of the world's great mysteries.''

And then he looked at her again, smiling. ''Your father was here, by the way. And the tabloid quoted him accurately. He knew of the wealth that was beneath this ground, just as you do. And now I think you have more than one reason to try to find it.''

''I don't know what you're talking about,'' Lyndsay said, growing uneasy. ''This is just more craziness and daydreams and it's too early in the morning to be having this conversation. I'm going back to bed.''

She turned to go, and almost bumped into Jed.

''Who are you talking to?'' he asked, looking around.

''Gabe,'' she answered, turning back to where the older man had stood. But he was no longer there.

She looked around, trying to part the darkness with her eyes. ''He was here a minute ago,'' she insisted.

Jed chuckled softly. ''I hate it when he does that. An old Indian trick, I guess.''

''I guess,'' Lyndsay agreed, still uneasy.

Jed encircled her waist from behind, drawing her back against him gently. It was impossible not to relax into his embrace. A sense of rightness and contentment filled her.

She leaned her head back against his shoulder. His breath brushed her hair.

''You shouldn't have gotten up,'' she said.

"I was cold without you. Besides, I wanted to tell you something."

She tilted her head around to look at him.

"I might have given you the wrong impression last night," he said, "when I was talking about what I'd do with the money. My grandfather said it belonged to the tribe. I think it belongs to whoever can find it, and I never planned to give the first dollar of it away. What I want to do," he said, drawing a breath, "is fly. With my share of the money, I'd buy an air-charter service in some exotic place like Sri Lanka or Borneo."

She raised an eyebrow. "You'd spend found money on a business, when you'd never have to work again in your life."

"All part of the plan," he assured her, "to keep the government off my back. You know how Uncle Sam feels about found money."

Lyndsay was thoughtful for a moment. It occurred to her that if he had never led her to believe his motives were so altruistic, she might have had a much harder time getting up the courage to tell him the truth. And in that way, he had done her a favor.

She laughed softly, lifting her hand to caress his cheek. "You know something? I'm glad you're still a scoundrel. Virtuous people bore me."

"I don't think either one of us have to worry about an excess of virture," Jed answered, and dropped a kiss into her hair. "But I've got to tell you, I'm awfully glad you're on my side."

Lyndsay smiled and leaned back against him, closing her eyes contentedly. ''Same here,'' she murmured.

She only hoped it would last.

Chapter Fourteen

For the next week they worked side by side, shoveling out the canyon wall. It became more and more apparent to Lyndsay that they were moving through the results of earth that had shifted rather recently—within the last few hundred years at any rate, which lent credence to Jed's theory that the treasure had originally been hidden in a cave that time had sealed over.

At first the pleasure was simply in working with Jed, in watching him, bare-chested in the sun, swing a pickax or use a shovel, and knowing that he was watching her, too, with the same kind of intense and energizing pleasure; in tasting his kiss, long and hot, in the middle of day and smelling their intermingled sweat and feeling the slide of oiled muscles beneath her hands; in making love with him at night under the stars, long and slow, and falling into the deep and for the most part dreamless sleep of well-earned exhaustion. But before long she, too, was drawn into the excitement of believing, however much she tried to fight it. The treasure was there, she knew it. And the fact that they would be sharing it, instead of dividing it, only made her feel twice as rich.

On the seventh day of digging they found the second coin.

Jed threw his shovel down and roared with triumph; he caught Lyndsay by the waist and whirled her around until, squealing with laughter, she begged him to stop. Work was suspended for the rest of that day, and Lyndsay wanted to share in Jed's enthusiasm, she truly did, but she couldn't, not entirely.

The fact was, what they had found was not a coin.

It was certainly a match for the first one they had found, though, being more deeply protected in the ground, not quite as badly eroded. The edges were still round, and some of the carving was visible, but it was perfectly clear to Lyndsay that the United States government had never minted anything like this.

"Look," she insisted, holding it out to Jed. "It even has a hole drilled in the top. And this figure that's etched here—it looks like a woman to me. It took the United States two centuries to consider putting a woman on their coinage and by that time it was hardly even worth the silver it was stamped on."

She shook her head slowly, still frowning over it. "No, this is some kind of ornament, it has to be.

Who would even make coins this big? God, I wish I knew more about the nineteenth century.''

They were back at the campsite, sitting outside at the folding table they used for meals. The table contained nothing now except the two pieces of gold, lying side by side atop the treasure map. Jed was sprawled back comfortably in his chair, drinking beer from the bottle. Lyndsay's beer was open but untouched in her hand.

"How much do you think it's worth?" Jed said.

He sat with one arm crossed on his chest, the beer bottle held casually in his other hand. He looked relaxed and his tone was one of only mildest curiosity, but energy crackled from him like a live wire. Lyndsay loved that about him, she didn't want to take it from him. She wanted to believe, for his sake and hers, in happy endings.

But something wouldn't quite let her.

She reached for the newest of the coins, weighing it in her hand. "This? God, it's hard to say. There's probably an ounce of gold in it. Of course we don't know how pure it is. But then there's the rarity factor—some collector could easily pay ten thousand dollars for it as it sits. Those guys are truly weird. But if we could identify it, actually date it..." She turned it over in her hand, having a hard time keeping her own excitement under check now. "It could be priceless. Museums would bid on it, collectors would fight over it..."

And then she shrugged, deliberately reining her enthusiasm as she replaced the coin on the map. "Of course it's probably going to turn out to be a button off some Spanish soldier's breastplate or something. Not," she had to add, fighting down the spark of anticipation again, "that that would be anything to sneeze at."

"So what you're telling me," Jed said, pretending thoughtfulness, "is that these two coins here, that we dug up in a week's work, are in the worst-case scenario worth more than I made all last year breaking my butt twelve hours a day—but we shouldn't get too excited because they're not U.S. mint?"

"It's just that... Don't you see, this throws the whole story off! If the coins in the chest aren't government issue then maybe there's no chest. And if there's no chest, maybe there's no treasure. Maybe there never was."

Jed started to laugh, softly. "Lord, lady. I've never seen anybody work so damn hard to be cynical. You're sitting here looking at two coins worth ten grand a piece minimum and you *still* find something to complain about. What is it about you that won't let you believe anything good could be real?"

Lyndsay hesitated, but he was right. Maybe she *did* work too hard at being cynical. After all, Jed was real, and he was the best thing that had ever happened to her.

She smiled and reached for his hand. "Sorry," she said. "I guess I'm a little new at this dream-chasing business."

He winked at her and brought her fingers to his lips in a cavalier salute. "Stick around, kid," he said. "You'll learn something."

Lyndsay shared his grin and even let herself start to share his excitement, but she could not entirely dismiss the feeling that something just wasn't right about this. The only thing she couldn't figure out was what.

THAT NIGHT THEY MADE long, slow celebratory love, and afterward lay entwined in each other's arms with the moonlight streaming over them. And yes, it was easy to believe in the impossible. Delighted visions of caskets filled with gold kept drifting through Lyndsay's mind, and she counted them as she would sheep.

"Donovan," she murmured.

"Hmm?"

His fingers were winding strands of her hair into corkscrew curls, one after the other. It was a lovely, soothing caress.

"I was just wondering..." And she knew no other way to say it except straight out. "If you had to choose between me and the treasure, which would it be?"

He dropped a kiss onto her hair. "I don't have to choose," he said. "I'm going to have both."

And then he hesitated. "What about you?"

Lyndsay grinned and wrapped her arms around him, snuggling close. "I'm going to have both, too."

And for the first time she actually believed it was possible. Or maybe she, like Donovan, simply wanted to believe it.

THAT NIGHT SHE HAD the strangest dream of all. Perhaps it was because she was still, subconsciously, trying to turn triumph into defeat, or perhaps her sleeping mind was trying to make sense of something that was in essence completely irrational.

In it she was walking through the canyon and it looked much like it had the day she had first seen it. The Widowmaker was in prominence, the stream forked just where she remembered it. It was sunset and the sky looked as though it had been painted with a brush.

She walked past the site where she and Jed were excavating. Their shovels and picks were stuck upright in the ground, the rest of the equipment neatly covered with a tarp. The site looked just as it always did after work was finished for the day.

A voice spoke behind her, vaguely familiar even though she couldn't see the speaker. "This is the wrong place, you know," it said.

Disappointment stabbed through her middle. "No. It can't be. We found the coins."

The voice was pleasant but firm. "You're close, but what you seek isn't here. Turn around."

Lyndsay looked around, and it was the most amazing thing. The sun was just setting over the opposite wall of the canyon, and was poised suspended so that a beam of light was caught in the crack between two rocks. With the twilight floor of the canyon forming a perfect backdrop, the sunbeam shot across the canyon and struck the opposite wall about ten feet from where they were digging.

The voice was amused. "Did you ever wonder why it's called Whispering Rock?"

"Because the wind, blowing through that crack, makes a sound like whispering," she said.

"It was spring when I was here," he replied. "Now it's summer."

"Joshua?"

And when she opened her eyes she was surprised to find she had spoken the word out loud.

The dream lingered and was so incredibly vivid that during the day, at odd moments, she found herself scanning the opposite wall of the canyon, looking for the two rocks that looked like one, with the odd-shaped crack where they met.

She never found it.

THREE DAYS LATER Jed's shovel struck something hard and metallic. It was like an epiphany, every detail of the moment etched stark and clear on the fabric of memory: the dull *clunk* of the shovel against metal reverberated like a church bell, and the everyday chatterings and chirping of the wildlife around them suddenly took on form and rhythm, like a rising chorus. The sun flared brilliantly, the air grew crystalline. The moment of truth was at hand.

Without saying a word, Lyndsay moved forward with a whisk and a trowel, brushing the dirt away, outlining the shape. It was definitely a strongbox, riveted with iron, of a style appropriate to the eighteenth or nineteenth century. It measured approximately eighteen by twelve inches, though its depth remained concealed underground.

Not very big, Lyndsay thought. *Please, let this be it. Don't let him be disappointed.*

Jed worked beside her on his knees, moving earth with his trowel and prying away stubborn rocks with a small pick. His face was tight and he hadn't said a word.

Fifteen years, Lyndsay thought. *A lifetime of hoping, three generations of believing...* When the box was almost free and fully exposed she sat back on her heels and let Jed finish the job. Her fists were clenched and she repeated one word over and over to herself, *Please, please, please...*

She was pleading, not for herself, but for the man she loved.

Jed lifted the box from the ground. Lyndsay could almost hear his heart beating.

Jed paused with his hands on the lid, and looked at her. There was a moment when she thought he almost didn't want to know what was inside. The expectation was agony. He turned back to the box.

The leather hinges had rotted away and the lid lifted easily. A large beetle crawled out, but that was all.

The box was completely empty.

Lyndsay supposed there had been other such moments in her life. The moment she had read the letter turning her down for the only job she ever wanted. The day her father died. Segments of time attenuated in horror, frozen in denial; a dividing line drawn down the center of the life. Before this moment there was hope. Afterward, there was none.

The silence seemed to go on forever. Even the birds stopped chirping. Not a breeze stirred the air.

Then Jed said in a dull, flat tone, "The one thing I didn't allow for. I never figured someone would get there before me."

He let the lid fall closed again and got to his feet. He walked a few feet away and stood with his back to her. Just looking at him caused Lyndsay's muscles to twist with pain. This couldn't be happening. God, why was this happening?

Her throat felt like dust, and she was surprised she could even make a sound. "No," she said.

He didn't turn around. It didn't matter.

"No one was here before you. The treasure was never in this box."

She dropped her eyes to the closed, battle-scarred strongbox. She simply couldn't look at Jed.

"Joshua buried the map," she said quietly. "That was the only thing he ever had, and that was what was in this box. The kid—the cowboy—he saw him do it. He lied when he said he took the map off Joshua's body. He took it out of the strongbox and spent the rest of his life trying to find out what it was. Why it was worth dying for."

Jed turned around slowly. "How do you know that?" he demanded quietly. And then he shouted, *"How the hell could you possibly know that?"*

But Lyndsay had no answer.

Jed turned on his heel and walked away.

LYNDSAY WAITED until almost dawn, hoping he would come back and do something, or say something, to stop her. But he didn't.

She understood what he was going through, and she understood his need to go through it alone. And in a way, it was easier this way. Her choices were so much clearer.

What a fool she'd been. All that talk of dreams and possibilities, and, God, he'd made it sound so convincing. She'd wanted so badly to believe, for his sake even more than hers. But buried treasure, for heaven's sake. Wouldn't she ever learn?

The truth was, she *had* known better. She had simply been blinded by love. And she probably still was.

Jed had taken to leaving the map, with the coins folded inside, in a dresser drawer inside the trailer while they worked during the day. Lyndsay had scolded him for that but he had just laughed and reminded her that the only person he'd ever worried about stealing the map was her.

And even as she was tucking the map and the coins into her duffel, even as she slipped the strap of the bag over her shoulder and stepped out into the dawn, she was waiting for Jed to come and catch her in the act. Hoping.

Jed had the keys to the truck with him, so she started walking north out of the canyon toward Gabe's camp. She walked for a long time. Maybe it was the eerie, lightless quality of the dawn, maybe her aching and distracted mind distorted time, but she seemed to remember Gabe's camp being much closer. She didn't see how she could have walked past it, and she began to worry he might have moved his camp, or even left the canyon. Then headlights struck her from behind and pinned her in their glare.

Lyndsay's heart skipped several beats even though she knew it couldn't possibly be Jed—mostly because that truck of his made enough noise to wake the dead and she hadn't even heard the vehicle that crept up behind her. She turned, squinting, and Gabe Blackwater waved to her from a Jeep a few yards back.

She waited until he pulled up beside her.

"You're up early," she said.

"I could say the same about you," he replied cheerfully. "I was on my way into town and like to get my traveling done before the heat of the day."

"I was just going to ask you for a ride."

"Well, isn't that a happy coincidence?"

As Lyndsay got inside and they drove off, she thought it was somewhat odd that he didn't inquire about her bag, or what she was doing on foot out in the canyon alone. Or perhaps he was just being polite.

She decided to save them both some awkwardness. "Tell Jed that I'll leave him a money order in care of general delivery in town here. He'll know what it's for. It'll probably take a couple of weeks."

Gabe nodded, his pleasant expression never changing. "So you're leaving us. What a shame. I thought you would be the one."

She looked at him in the dark. "The one to what?"

"Prove your father was right. Prove us all right."

Lyndsay leaned her head back against the seat, overwhelmed with defeat. "Please, Gabe. I'm too tired for this."

They drove in silence for a while. Lyndsay felt the terrain change from dirt to gravel to blacktop. She opened her eyes just as the sky was starting to turn lavender, and the first signs of civilization appeared.

Gabe began to speak as though continuing a conversation that had only been briefly interrupted—a habit of his to which Lyndsay was not certain she would ever grow accustomed.

"Joshua was one of those who believed in the legacy of the Old Ones, you know. Of course he had good reason. He also had a theory, that originally a map was left with each of the five civilized tribes—whether this is true or not we may never know, but it does make a certain amount of sense. Or perhaps the Creek, through some twist of history lost in time, were chosen to be the keepers of the secret for all the tribes. That, too, we'll never know."

Lyndsay listened, riveted by his words even though logically nothing he was saying made sense to her, even though it didn't even concern her or have any place in her life now at all.... She listened, because on some level it *did* matter.

"You may remember the stories about the Cherokee burying their tribal valuables before they were herded off on the Trail of Tears, always planning to come back for them when they were settled in their new home. The Creek weren't quite as rich a tribe as the Cherokee, but they had their valuables, too, that they were afraid to take when they were sent to Indian territory. So they hid them from the white man, always planning to come back. Of course, once they got to Oklahoma they were too busy trying to survive to worry about what they left behind or, in most cases, to even remember.

"But Joshua knew where the most valuable possession that had ever fallen into Creek hands was hidden. It was so valuable, in fact, that if word ever got out about what he had, not only would his life, and the lives of his family, be in danger, but there'd be war among the tribes, not to mention with the white man. But Joshua knew when he returned to his people with chests full of gold, questions would be asked. So he put out the story of negotiating with the United States government for compensation for their lands.

"He knew the chances of making it out alive were not good, so he hid the map in a small cave that he thought was the entrance to the treasure tunnel. It was actually just an anteroom, which explains why you found those few coins that shifted during the earthquake. You could have dug for years in that spot and never entered the main tunnel though. The designers were ingenious about disguising the access points. But then they had to be—they were protecting the legacy of an entire civilization."

"How do you know that?" Lyndsay demanded. Her heart was beating hard and the uneasiness that pressed down on her was almost smothering. "How could you possibly know that?"

The Jeep had stopped in front of the small motel at the edge of town. Lyndsay knew she should get out of the vehicle—she should *run* out—but she couldn't make herself move.

Gabe smiled at her. "Of course, if only he had waited a month, and watched the sun set, the light would have led him right to the door. But it probably all worked out for the best in the end, don't you think?"

Lyndsay suddenly remembered the voice in her dream, and knew where she had heard it before.

She was out of the Jeep without realizing she had moved her legs. She backed one step away, staring at him.

"Who *are* you?" she demanded hoarsely.

Gabe lifted his hand from the steering wheel in a wave. "If you need a ride back, you let me know," he said. And he drove off.

In a daze, Lyndsay walked into the motel office and asked for a room. The woman she had awakened in order to do so was sleepy and disgruntled and looked at Lyndsay suspiciously, but Lyndsay was barely aware of it.

She entered her room without noticing what it looked like, and fell on the bed. There she slept soundly and dreamlessly, for the first time since coming to Colorado.

IT WAS MIDAFTERNOON when Lyndsay awoke, half-convinced she had dreamed the entire episode with Gabe. She only wished she could look back upon the events of the past twenty-four hours as nothing more than a nightmare now gone, but reality settled into the pit of her stomach like a cold, bruising fist.

She showered and changed her clothes, and it was then that she realized there was no telephone in her room. In a motel with more cockroaches than rooms she supposed that was not too unusual, but she was irritated by the inconvenience until she noticed the pay phone outside the office.

She put a coin in and dialed collect.

Jeffrey answered after half a dozen rings. He sounded surly and Lyndsay suspected she had awakened him—not surprising, given his proclivities. But he snapped quickly into alertness when he heard her name and accepted the charges with dispatch.

"Damn it, Lyndsay, where the hell have you been? Do you know how long I've been trying to reach you?"

"Listen, Jeffrey. You remember a certain item we talked about last time? I have it, and I want you to broker it for me. Top dollar. I also have a couple of collectibles a discriminating art lover might appreciate—for the right price."

Jeffrey hesitated, then released a low breath. "You actually *found* something?"

"That's right." She kept her tone bland.

"Let me guess. We're not talking about potsherds here, are we?"

"That's right."

Another brief, though charged silence. Lyndsay could practically see the wheels turning in his head.

"All right," Jeffrey said, "you listen to me. You're not going to believe what *I* found out. I started looking up old records, and guess what? There never was any negotiation for payment of lands, Joshua Running Horse never collected a cent. What he *did* do was make a trip to Alabama and ask permission of a farmer to look for some tribal artifacts—the farm was on what used to be Creek land. Naturally the farmer scoped him out from a distance, just in case he turned up something more than artifacts. But all he found, according to this farmer, was a piece of leather with symbols on it.''

''The map,'' Lyndsay whispered. She suddenly became aware of how hot the sun was. Perspiration broke out on her forehead and her knees felt weak.

''Exactly. So, in the classic good news/bad news fashion, we either have a map that leads nowhere, or the key to the accumulated wealth of the entire Creek nation.''

''Or even more.''

She spoke the words without meaning to say anything at all out loud, and they must not have been particularly intelligible because Jeffrey said, ''What?''

She tried to focus. ''Nothing.''

''So here's the situation, babe, and I'd think twice before giving away that map if I were you . . .''

But the rest of his words faded away as a ghostly reflection appeared beside her own in the plastic shield that surrounded the telephone. Her throat went dry, her heart started to pound.

She said hoarsely, ''I'll call you back,'' and dropped the receiver into its cradle.

She turned around to face Jed.

His face was unshaven, his eyes bloodshot, his jaw set. Lyndsay thought her heart would break, just looking at him.

Jed's fingers closed on her forearm, tightly. ''Do you have a room?''

Lyndsay swallowed hard and nodded. She led the way to her room and he did not once slacken his steel grip on her arm. Inside, she pulled away and turned to face him. Not just her heart, but everything inside her was breaking, shattering into a million pieces.

She raised her chin and kept her voice steady. "I wasn't going to keep any of the money, in case you're interested. I can always make a living, but you—between the map and the coins, you had enough to buy at least one plane, if you found a broker who knew what she was doing. I did. No charge."

His eyes were as dark as the bottom of a lake, his face expressionless. "You think that's why I'm here. To recover stolen property."

Her heart started thumping, slow and hard but she tried not to let it show. Her voice was cool. "Aren't you?"

"No, damn it!" The icy layer of his control broke and anger flared in his eyes. "I don't care what you do with the map—hell what difference does it make to me now? What difference has it *ever* made? What I care about is that you thought you had to do anything!"

He stepped forward and grabbed her arm again, giving it a little shake. Frustration and fury and need and demand churned in his eyes, tightening his face. "Damn it, Lyndsay, I don't need you to take care of me! I'm not your father. I don't need you to think for me or protect me or clean up after me, do you understand that?''

He released her arm and half turned away, drawing in a sharp breath as he ran his fingers through his hair. "I won't deny it was a shock, losing out after coming so close. Maybe I shouldn't have walked out on you like that but I won't apologize for it. I needed to deal with it in my own way, I needed time to figure out some things.... Hell, you live your life a certain way for so long and then suddenly the things you've built it around aren't there anymore and naturally you've got some thinking to do. Some priorities to set."

It was with a very great effort that Lyndsay kept her voice steady. "And did you?"

He turned to look at her. The anger was gone now, and his expression was quiet, sober and honest. "You asked me once what I'd choose if I had to choose between you and the treasure. What I wanted to tell you was that the only treasure that ever mattered was you. Looking for the gold was just something to do until you came along, and I'm not willing to lose you to greed or money or fear. That's what I came here to tell you."

Lyndsay fought the tears that flooded her chest and stung her eyes, but she couldn't quite control the trembling of her voice as she said, "I'm glad." And she moved into his arms.

Jed held her tightly, so tightly she thought her ribs would crack, but no more tightly than she held him.

When she lifted her face, seeking his lips, he caught her head gently in his hands and looked into her eyes.

"No more secrets," he said quietly. "I told you why I ran away. Why did you?"

She dropped her eyes. "I wasn't running from you," she said brokenly. "I never wanted to leave you."

With a gentle pressure of his fingers, he made her look at him again. "You can't run away from yourself, either, Lyns."

Helplessness filled her. She didn't know what to say.

"I don't know whether your father was psychic or not," Jed said gently, "but you are. Aren't you?"

"No," she whispered.

But she couldn't squirm away from his gaze, quiet and steady, patient and receptive. "Oh, Donovan, I don't know," she said miserably. "It's all so confusing, so crazy. I don't believe in half the stuff that's been happening to me but I can't deny it happened, and—it scares me. Not because it's happening, but because I don't understand it and I don't know what to do about it."

"Ah, honey." Tenderly Jed drew her against his shoulder, releasing a slow breath into her hair. "I don't, either, but maybe together we can figure it out."

Those were the sweetest words Lyndsay had ever heard.

Their mouths met, their hands caressed. What flowed and blossomed between them was more than affection, more than desire; it was commitment, deep and sure, for better or worse, time without end.

"I love you, lady," Jed said huskily when at last they parted. "And I want us to make a life together, whatever it takes. But I need to hear you say it. If things had worked out differently—if you'd had to choose—what would it have been? Me or the treasure?"

Lyndsay tilted her head back to look at him. It was still a wonderful feeling to be able to do that. She looked at him for a long time, and then she said softly, "I don't have to choose. I have them both." Then she took a breath.

"Jed, I know where the treasure is."

IT WAS a very strange drive back to the canyon. The silence was comfortable and warm, but the fact that they could be silent at all was amazing. They had so much to say to each other. But they also had a lifetime in which to say it.

They were about to embark upon the biggest adventure of their lives, but they were as relaxed as though they were merely going out to dinner. Perhaps it was because they had discovered something more powerful than gold, more alluring than buried treasure.

At one point Jed inquired casually, "How'd you get into town, anyway? Hitchhike?"

She shook her head, fingers encircling his. "Gabe gave me a lift in his Jeep."

Jed glanced at her. "Gabe doesn't have a Jeep. As a matter of fact..." And he frowned a little. "That's funny. I've never seen a vehicle of any kind at his camp, but they had to get into the canyon somehow."

Lyndsay felt a little chill go down her spine, and she sat up straighter. "Jed," she said slowly, "could we stop by Gabe's camp first? I think he should be there when we open the tunnel."

Jed didn't seem surprised by the request, and agreed readily.

He was, however, surprised when they drove to Gabe's campsite and found it deserted. Not only was it deserted, but it was overgrown by sagebrush and ground cover to the extent that it was clear no one had even walked there, much less camped there, in years.

At first Jed assumed he had mistaken the campsite and spent half an hour driving up and down the canyon. Finally he returned to the original site and they both got out of the truck, walking the ground and looking for signs of recent habitation.

"This is impossible," Jed said for what must have been the twelfth time. He slapped his hat on his thigh in annoyance. "I know this canyon like the back of my hand and this was where he was camped. How could there not even be a sign of a campfire?"

"Maybe because he was never here at all."

Jed stared at her. "Come on, Lyns! You ate the man's food, you rode in his car, you had God knows how many conversations with him, just like I did. What are you trying to say?"

"Just..." She hesitated, then added thoughtfully, "Donovan...what was your great-grandmother's name? Joshua's wife?"

"Mary," he answered. "But I don't see what that has to do with—"

And then understanding dawned and he shook his head adamantly. "No. That's where I draw the line. Lyndsay, that's crazy!"

But Lyndsay was remembering the twinkle in Gabe's eyes.

Ever see any ghosts?

This canyon is filled with them.

She smiled. "It doesn't matter," she told Jed, and linked her arm through his. "Come on, let's go."

THEY WATCHED THE SUN set through the crack where the two rocks joined, and merely followed the arrow of light. It took Jed less than one minute to discover the pressure points in the rocky face of the opposite wall.

The rock pivoted open like a door, emitting a rush of cool, stale air—air that had been trapped inside the earth a thousand years or more.

Afterward Lyndsay would be amazed at how calmly they accepted all of this, as though it were a movie they were watching together, or a game of scavenger hunt or hide-and-seek. She supposed they were both in some kind of shock. None of it seemed quite real.

She let Jed go first. It was, after all, his treasure.

"Be careful," she warned. "The air is probably bad."

He was standing at the entrance to a cave which, beyond the four-foot-tall rock door, was approximately six feet high, eight feet wide. Lyndsay was standing behind him and couldn't see all the way inside, although occasionally she could see Jed's flashlight bounce off distant walls.

His voice sounded odd as he replied, "Don't worry. I won't have to go far."

He bent down and picked something up. When he turned, he was carrying a tarnished chest of about two feet square, ornately carved in what might very well be silver. His arm muscles bulged with the strain, and he couldn't lift it much above his knees. He carried it only a few feet outside the entrance and set it on the ground, breathing hard.

Lyndsay dropped to her knees beside him, her hand lightly stroking the metal. Definitely silver, or silver alloy, and looking vaguely familiar to her. It had no lock.

She looked at Jed. He looked back.

"Shall we open it?" she said.

And he smiled. "Why not?"

Lyndsay lifted the lid. And they both fell back in silence.

No pirate's cache ever created by Hollywood was so dramatic. For a moment Lyndsay thought she was actually looking at stage props, costume jewelry, but then she knew she wasn't because she had seen it all before... somewhere.

The chest was filled to the brim with tangled chains of gold and silver, loose cut stones, polished gold disks, thick hammered bracelets set with amethysts and onyx, intricately fashioned rings worked in pearls and rubies and crystal-clear emeralds. Lyndsay saw a diamond as big as her thumbnail. She saw stones she couldn't even identify, but whose luster and glow shouted of the work of an artist of extraordinary skill.

Just what she could see represented enough wealth to keep two people living in extraordinary style for the rest of their lives. And there were layers upon layers beneath that.

It was instinctual and they moved as one, first to touch the pieces, then to thrust their hands into the chest, to feel the sensual thrill of stone upon flesh. To know it was real. To know it was theirs.

She pulled out a gold chain and held it up to the light. It was heavy, studded with brilliant red stones and supporting a carved medallion with the profile of a woman and hieroglyphs like none she had ever seen. It took Lyndsay a long time to absorb what she held in her hand, what filled the chest beside her. Not just stones and precious metal, but a whole culture, heretofore unknown, artistry beyond compare, each piece unique and without precedent.

"My God," she said softly. She couldn't take her eyes off the piece. "My God."

"Lyndsay."

Something about his tone captured her attention, dragging her gaze from the necklace to his face. It still had that odd, stunned look about it, though his hands, too, were filled with jewels.

"There are dozens of these boxes in there," he said. "Hundreds of them stacked up against the walls. And the walls—the tunnel—it goes on forever. We could spend a lifetime just opening up what's inside."

The implication washed over Lyndsay like a tidal wave. A series of tidal waves. It was a long time before she could speak.

"This is not Creek," she said. Her voice sounded odd, hoarse and stiff.

"No." Jed's voice, too, seemed strained, reaching her as though from far away. "Lyns...it looks as though your father was right all along."

"Anasazi," she whispered.

"Or," he agreed soberly, "something even older— a civilization the world has forgotten."

Lyndsay closed her fingers around the heavy gold chain she held and brought it to her face, closing her eyes tightly against the sting of tears. "Oh, Dad," she whispered. "You were right. All the time...you were right."

Jed's hand slipped around her neck in a gesture of comfort and understanding.

She opened her eyes, smiling through her tears. "It just doesn't seem fair, you know. He should have made the discovery, not us. He would have been vindicated."

Tenderly Jed brushed a drop of moisture from her cheek. "I don't think that would have mattered to him. I think the only person he ever needed to believe in him was you."

"How can you know that?"

He smiled. "We dreamers and sunchasers have a lot in common."

And then his expression sobered. "Lyndsay—those boxes. They might not all contain jewelry."

She nodded slowly, gripped once again by the wider implications of what they had found. "If this civilization was as technologically advanced as—as Dad, and others, believed . . ." Her eyes widened as she looked at Jed. "Donovan, I don't think we can take the responsibility of letting the world in on this. Who knows what's in that cave?"

"The world is full of crazies," he agreed. "If people find out about this . . ."

But he didn't have to finish. They looked at each other for a long time, and without saying a word, they knew what they had to do.

AN HOUR LATER the door was back in place. The canyon wall, to the casual observer, looked undisturbed. The treasure map was sealed inside, but one chest—the one Jed had first brought out—they kept.

"You know I'll have to come back someday," Lyndsay said.

What she had seen inside had only tantalized the archaeologist in her, for Jed had been right: not all the boxes contained jewelry. Though she knew she might not ever explain the mysteries contained in that tunnel, or even fully explore them in her lifetime, she also knew she'd never rest easy until she had at least tried.

Jed slipped his arm around her waist. "And you know I'll be with you."

They spent another moment gazing at the canyon wall, pondering the enormity of what they had discovered.

"I hope we don't have to break any of it down," he said, with surprising sentimentality. "It's all so beautiful."

Lyndsay smiled at him. "If we sell one piece it will be more than enough to live on comfortably the rest of our lives. Enough," she added, "to set up that air-charter service of yours anyplace in the world."

Kneeling on the ground beside the chest, he smiled up at her. "Not before we take an extended trip to Egypt. You might even want to call it a honeymoon."

Lyndsay felt the breath leave her lungs and she sank to her knees beside him. "Oh, Jed, do you mean it?"

He threaded his fingers through her hair, cupping her face. "Only if you think you'd like to marry me."

"I would!" she whispered as their lips met. "I would!"

They broke apart at last, laughing, holding each other, sitting on the ground beside the open casket of treasure. They stayed that way for a long time.

Then Jed turned back once again, to secure the lid of the box for transportation back to the trailer. He hesitated.

"Look at this," he said, pulling out one piece. "Isn't that something? Like those Chinese rings. I was always pretty good at those."

Everything inside Lyndsay seemed to freeze, then flow together slowly in a sweet golden warmth, like honey in the sunshine. The piece he held up was a pair of interlinked bracelets braided in silver and gold, studded with topaz.

"It's a bracelet, I think," he said. "Hold out your arm."

She hesitated. "There's no clasp. It'll never fit over my hand. It doesn't open."

"Of course it does," he said, and took her arm. "For the right person."

The bracelet opened to the deft touch of his fingers, and he fastened it on her wrist.

Lyndsay looked at the bracelet in muted wonder and awe. Then, with a muffled cry of joy, she threw her arms around Jed's neck and hugged him hard, holding him, loving him. Jed laughed in surprise and pleasure, and hugged her back.

High on the opposite wall of the canyon, silhouetted against the glow of the setting sun, Lyndsay thought she saw a Native American man, smiling and waving to her.

She waved back.

Take 4 bestselling love stories FREE

Plus get a FREE surprise gift!

Special Limited-time Offer

Mail to Harlequin Reader Service®

> 3010 Walden Avenue
> P.O. Box 1867
> Buffalo, N.Y. 14269-1867

YES! Please send me 4 free Harlequin American Romance® novels and my free surprise gift. Then send me 4 brand-new novels every month, which I will receive months before they appear in bookstores. Bill me at the low price of $2.71 each plus 25¢ delivery and applicable sales tax, if any.*That's the complete price and—compared to the cover prices of $3.50 each—quite a bargain! I understand that accepting the books and gift places me under no obligation ever to buy any books. I can always return a shipment and cancel at any time. Even if I never buy another book from Harlequin, the 4 free books and the surprise gift are mine to keep forever.

154 BPA AJJF

Name _____ (PLEASE PRINT)

Address _____ Apt. No. _____

City _____ State _____ Zip _____

Harlequin is proud to present our best authors and their best books. Always the best for your reading pleasure!

Throughout 1993, Harlequin will bring you exciting books by some of the top names in contemporary romance!

In July
look for
The Ties That Bind by

Shannon wanted him seven days a week....

Dark, compelling, mysterious Garth Sheridan was no mere boy next door—even if he did rent the cottage beside Shannon Raine's.

She was intrigued by the hard-nosed exec, but for Shannon it was all or nothing. Either break the undeniable bonds between them . . . or tear down the barriers surrounding Garth and discover the truth.

Don't miss THE TIES THAT BIND ...
wherever Harlequin books are sold.

BOB3

Fifty red-blooded, white-hot, true-blue hunks from every State in the Union!

Beginning in May, look for MEN MADE IN AMERICA! Written by some of our most popular authors, these stories feature fifty of the strongest, sexiest men, each from a different state in the union!

Two titles available every other month at your favorite retail outlet.

In July, look for:

CALL IT DESTINY by Jayne Ann Krentz (Arizona)
ANOTHER KIND OF LOVE by Mary Lynn Baxter
(Arkansas)

In September, look for:

DECEPTIONS by Annette Broadrick (California)
STORMWALKER by Dallas Schulze (Colorado)

You won't be able to resist MEN MADE IN AMERICA!

Where do you find hot Texas nights, smooth Texas charm and dangerously sexy cowboys?

EVEN THE NIGHTS ARE BETTER
by Margot Dalton

Second chance—Texas style!

Vernon Trent has loved Carolyn Townsend ever since they were in first grade. When the widowed Carolyn needs help, she turns to Vern and he gets a second chance to win her love. But if Carolyn finds out Vern is actually responsible for her problem, will she ever forgive him?

CRYSTAL CREEK reverberates with the exciting rhythm of Texas. Each story features the rugged individuals who live and love in the Lone Star State. And each one ends with the same invitation...

Y'ALL COME BACK...REAL SOON!
Don't miss *EVEN THE NIGHTS ARE BETTER*
by Margot Dalton
Available in July wherever Harlequin books are sold.